The Wagons of Perro Loco

To JUANITA & Bob

Live Long & Happy

J. C. 'Doc' Pendland

The Wagons of Perro Loco

And Other Short Stories

JL "Doc" Pendland

To order additional copies of this book, contact:
Xlibris Corporation
1-888-795-4274
www.Xlibris.com
Orders@Xlibris.com
75380

Contents

A Note From The Author

Growing up in northern Oklahoma during the 1940's and 1950's, the kids in my town looked forward to Saturday afternoon matinees at the Palace, or Rivoli theatres.

No matter what the main feature was, there were always two cartoons, and at least one serial (on today's television it's called a mini-series). A movie theatre would show one episode each week. There may be as little as two parts, or as many as fifteen. No matter what the number, we kids wanted to catch them all. At school on Mondays, we discussed what had happened on the big screen, and disagreed over our predictions for the next episode.

Of course, there were the science fiction serials, Buck Rogers, Flash Gordon, Superman and others, but the ones that I *never* wanted to miss, were the western serials.

There was *The Lone Ranger* who was played by Bob Livingston, with Chief Thunder Cloud as *Tonto*.

Tom Mix, a Pennsylvania native, made the switch from silent movies to 'talkies' in *The Miracle Rider*. As a young man, he worked and rodeoed on the famous 101 Ranch, in Oklahoma, Indian Territory, not far from where I was raised.

The Sword of Zorro had twelve episodes. That masked man was awesome, with his sword and his riding skills. Nearly all of us boys had swords, made of sticks, boards, even pipe. Our moms were usually upset when they found our capes,(or masks) which, actually belonged in the bathroom, in the towel stack. Now they would have to be washed, again.

Lash Larue and *Whip Wilson* inspired countless numbers of rope whips, or just a strip off one of mom's towels, tied to the end of a limber stick. Upon mom's discovery of the torn towels, the sticks became switches, and were used for another purpose. But it was fun, anyway, while it lasted.

Western movies starring Bronco Billy Anderson, Tom Horn, Hoot Gibson, as well as other *shore 'nuff old time cowboys*, were even before my time, but, after my dad told me about them, I wanted to see them all.

Then came Rex Allen, Gene Autry, Johnny Mack Brown, William Boyd as Hopalong Cassidy, and (in my opinion the best 'yodeler' of all time) Roy Rogers.

Tim Holt was one of my favorites. He wasn't as big as most of the cowboy 'heroes', but was tough as any of 'em, and his six-gun would shoot twenty-five to thirty times, during a chase with a bad guy. Although born in Beverly Hills, he made his home in central Oklahoma, where he died in 1973.

One of the best cowboy actors of the '40's, '50's and '60's, in my 'expert' opinion, was Joel McCrea. The National Cowboy Hall of Fame, in Oklahoma City, thought so, too. In 1969, he was the first cowboy actor inducted, because of his contributions to the western film industry.

Over the years, the faces in the movies, and on television, changed. There was Henry Fonda, John Wayne, James Stewart, Clint Eastwood, James Arness and Michael Landon.

Now we have Sam Elliott, Robert Duval, Kevin Costner and Tom Selleck. Every time I see a western, even if I've seen it before, I'm reminded of the old ones.

It's the same when I read about Smoke Jensen, Longarm, the White Indian, or any number of today's 'heroes'. I like every book. Some better than others, but I like 'em all.

My dad worked at the local zinc smelter, mom at the glass plant. Dad liked to read mystery paperback books, such as the Mickey Spillane stories, but on occasion, he'd pick up a western book. I guess, that was when I started to like reading about the *old west*. I couldn't wait for him to finish those books, so I could have my turn.

Some of my favorite book characters remind me of the 'sidekicks', who were companions to the movie 'heroes'.

More so than the 'heroes', I believe I looked forward to seeing *those* characters, who were played by the likes of Smiley Burnette, Andy Devine, Walter Brennan and, of course the gripen'est, ugliest, whiner of all . . . . the crochety ol' 'Gabby' Hayes. He became one of the most memorable characters of western movies. No one would suspect he was actually born and raised in New York. He was great.

In most of my short stories, I have tried to incorporate similar characters. I feel that a little humor never hurt any story.

These are works of fiction. Some names may have been picked from past acquaintances, but only because 'I ain't quick 'nuff to think up new ones.'

Some research was done on a few of my stories, but most details 'jist rolled outten mah own haid.'

The Long Trip

**MEMPHIS,
GATEWAY TO THE WEST!
to
SAN FRANCISCO,
GATEWAY TO THE GOLD FIELDS!
IN JUST 22 DAYS!
ONLY $200!**

The sign over the Butterfield Overland Stage office was bright green, with gold trim and red lettering. The 9 passenger, Concord coach, setting in front of the station was intricately painted in the same colors. A matched set, six-horse hitch stood in the sun, freshly washed, groomed, and wearing harness of polished leather, studded with silver and brass. Departure times were written on the chalkboard, mounted by the door.

'Wow!' Robin thought to herself. *'What a beautiful stagecoach. It's going to be a wonderful trip, if I'll be riding in that, all the way to California.'*

She stepped inside the office, noted the cleanliness, and went directly to the barred window marked 'TICKETS'. "I'd like to buy a ticket to San Francisco, please," she told the pudgy man behind the counter.

"Passage is 200 dollars, young lady," he replied in a monotone voice. "The stage will leave on time at eight o'clock tomorrow morning. It would be wise to arrive at the station at least ten minutes early. Seating is based on a first come first served basis. The best seating is in the front of the coach. Next is the center, and the rear seat is the least comfortable. You'll have to hold your luggage, or place it under your seat, if there is room. You'll be charged extra, for any luggage which has to be stored elsewhere. If you have any of *that* type luggage, you need to check it in at least one hour prior to departure. The trip will take approximately 22 days. Much of the trip will be traversed in very hot weather. Light clothing is suggested. There will be many stops along the way, some as close as four miles apart, some as far as thirty. Privies are located at every stop, however, you are requested to remain on the coach, unless absolutely necessary, in which case, you are required to notify the conductor or the driver. Our coaches travel day and night. Most of your sleeping will be on board. Two weigh stations per day will provide meals to all passengers. Some of those will be boxed and waiting when the coach arrives. Do you have any questions?"

"Just one," answered Robin, with a smile, "How long did it take for you to memorize all that?"

The ticket manager exhaled, and looked up at Robin. "I'm sorry ma'm, it's just my job. It's required for me to inform the passengers of the rules. Many of them can't read. This way everyone knows what they are."

Robin had noticed the man's brass name tag, pinned to his shirt, and said, "That's alright Mr. Simms, you're doing a fine job." She paid him with the cash she was holding, picked up her ticket, and continued, "I'll be here on time, you have a good day."

Robin Elaine Hopkins was nineteen years old. Raised on a dairy farm in West Virginia, she was a strong girl, not what many people would call pretty, but not a bad looking girl, either. At five and one half feet tall, she wasn't a dainty girl. Maybe it was all the fresh milk she had, as she was growing up, that made her teeth straight and her complexion smooth. She had attended school, which, luckily, was less than a mile from her home. After completing all eight grades, she went on to study bookkeeping with the treasurer of the township. Besides working on the farm, and studying bookkeeping, she worked four hours a day in the local mercantile.

Her father had left the farm, heading for the gold fields of California, a little more than two years before. Robin and her twin brother, Robert, were already doing most of the milking and the hay harvesting, so he told them and his wife, their step-mother, good bye and promised them he'd be back, . . . rich!

Her step-mother became very ill within the first six months after her father left. The illness progressed rapidly, and she died before Robin could get a letter to him. When she did send the letter, she told her father that she was moving to town, and that Robert was going to continue to run the farm.

Last week, Robin received a registered letter from her father. He had wired two thousand dollars to her bank account, and asked her to come to California. He had hit it rich, and wanted her to help him set up a business, and run it.

Robin only took her own savings from the bank, and bid good-bye to her home town. The other two thousand would remain, in case Robert needed it, or it could be retrieved, by wire, later.

The first part of her trip took seven days. It was a pleasant trip, by riverboat, down the Ohio River to the Mississippi, then down it to Memphis, Tennessee.

The weather was typical. Late spring, cool nights, pleasantly warm days. The rivers were running slightly high, which eliminated many sand bar hazards.

Robin had wired ahead to the Harper House, in downtown Memphis, for a room reservation, and had no problem settling in, for her last night in a good bed . . . . for a while.

During the late 1850's the United States government awarded a contract to John Butterfield, who would establish a mail route from two points on the Mississippi river, St. Louis, Missouri and Memphis, Tennessee, to San Francisco, California. The government insisted on a southern route, allowing travel to continue year round. Northern or mid-America routes would experience serious delays, due to weather problems, during winter months. Butterfield built stations at approximately twenty mile intervals. However, additional stops were made in towns, or at trading posts, for collection and distribution of mail.

800 stagecoaches were put into service, as well as 15,000 head of mules and horses. A driver and a conductor, which was actually an armed guard, was assigned to each coach.

U.S. Mail and passenger transport were the primary functions of the line. However, Army and other large payrolls were carried, but usually on specially arranged trips, with extra guards.

The breakfast was the best in town. Robin had the 'Harper House Special', which consisted of 'dry cured' ham, fresh eggs ('cooked to your desired taste'), hot biscuits, and 'red-eye' gravy. The butter was as delicious as that which Robin, herself, made back home. After eating all she could, she collected her valise, hired a young man to carry her suitcases to the station, and paid the hotel desk clerk. "Have a nice trip, ma'm," he said as she turned to leave. Robin just smiled and gave him a little wave.

When she arrived at the stage depot, a coach was parked in front. It was much less impressive than the Concord, parked there yesterday. This one had four strong mules hitched to it, and it had been very well used. Although there were to be nine passengers on the initial part of the trip, only one other passenger had arrived ahead of her, and the two of them selected the outside seats, on the front bench, facing toward the rear of the coach. Robin had paid four extra dollars for her suitcases to be carried in the rear boot, so the only thing she held on the coach, was her small valise.

"Yaaaaaa, Yaaaaaa! Git up there! Move yer asses!" The driver's voice was the loudest Robin had ever heard. The coach jerked into motion, and moved down the street, toward the ferry, which was waiting at the dock.

The mules never hesitated. As soon as the coach was on the ferry, the brakes were locked, lines were tied to anchor points on the coach, and it was moving out, into the Mississippi. By the time the ferry was tied tight, on the other side, the driver was screaming at the mules, again.

'He must have made that crossing a hundred times,' Robin thought, *'No wasted time at all. What sweet names he has for those mules . . . . I'll bet they have a few for him, too.'*

The first day of the trip was uneventful, with one exception. This was considered the 'delta' region of eastern Arkansas. Low and level, the land rolled past the coach windows. The road was smooth, and the travelers were in a good mood. *'Wonderful farming country'* Robin thought. *'However, if that river ever rose too high, countless miles would be underwater.'*

The man in the middle of the seat facing her spoke, "I've been told that, out there is some of the best farm land in this whole country. At one time, so they say, the Mississippi river flooded this land three or four times a year. The topsoil, washed away from upstream, was deposited in this area. I've heard that topsoil is as much as fifteen feet deep in parts of the region."

There is always one person in any group, who will argue or disagree with anyone, or everyone. "Now, that doesn't make any sense." It was the man next to Robin. "If it's fifteen feet deep, it can't be topsoil."

"I'm just making conversation." The first man replied. "I said I was 'told' that information. I didn't just make it up."

"Do you do any farming, sir?" Robin asked the man next to her.

"No, I don't, young lady, I sell books." he replied smartly, "but I do know some farmers."

"Well, now you know another one," she stared him directly in the eyes. "This is excellent farm land, sir. I, personally, have seen topsoil deeper than a man digs a grave, all of it deposited by flood waters. It's not polite to disagree, on a subject you know nothing about. It's going to be a long trip, and if you have information on a subject you *do* know about, you're welcome to share it, otherwise . . . ." She left her sentence hanging, but all the passengers knew the ending. Most were smiling, and the man who first told about the farmland winked at her and extended his hand. "I'm Captain Davis Jackson, ma'm, U.S. Army. I'm going all the way to San Francisco."

"Me too, Captain. I'm Robin Hopkins. I'm going to San Francisco to see my father." She was cautious to say anything that might cause anyone to think she, or her father may have money.

The coach was slowing down for the first way station. The conductor opened a small door behind the front seat, "Way station ahead, we'll be stopping for just a few minutes. Time for a privy stop. If you leave the coach, I'll need your name." The passengers were to find out that the first stop, each day, would take time for people to relieve themselves. It made sense, since most of them had eaten breakfast, a short time before.

The trip resumed in minutes, and continued thru to the fourth stop, which required a change of mules. The travelers were halfway through the first day. Four more stops and five hours later, the first, of many, legs of the trip was done.

At Brinkley, they changed coaches. The original one would return to Memphis, with east bound passengers. They were averaging about six miles an hour. That would be the average for the entire trip. The next four days would go a little slower. The stage line's schedule required a coach change every sixty miles. On particularly hard sections, maybe sooner, and longer intervals on smooth sections.

Two and one-half days later, the Concord pulled into Fort Smith. The conductor informed the passengers that there would be an unscheduled lay-over, until six a.m. the next morning. The St. Louis to Fort Smith coach would be arriving during the night, and some of those passengers would combine, with them, when the trip continued.

Robin inquired about a good hotel, and was directed to The River Inn. After getting a much needed bath, in the hotel bath house, Robin took a short nap in her room, then walked down the stairs to the dining room. Davis Jackson spotted her entering the room and asked her to join him.

"Sure," she responded. "Why have a change of scenery, now? I've been looking at your face for the last two days." She smiled and winked. "I'll have supper with you, if you'll promise not to snore, nod, or doze off. I've seen enough of that."

"Be careful, Miss Hopkins, I can tell some things about you, trying to get some sleep, too."

They enjoyed their meal, and walked, together to the river front. Davis started with "I've been told this is some of the best farm land in the country."

"Oh, no, not again" Robin complained. "I hope that book salesman isn't listening. I'd hate to have to protect you from him, again."

"Protect me? Why, Miss Hopkins, I was getting ready to throw that guy off the coach, but you got in the way." Captain Jackson started laughing and Robin couldn't help but join him.

"Please, Captain, call me Robin. In fact, at home my friends call me Rob, and my twin brother, Bob."

"Rob it is, then, if you'll call me Dave."

They walked and talked until nearly dark, returned to the hotel, and left word for a wake up call at four a.m.

The stagecoach left promptly at six the next morning. The Arkansas River crossing was not as smooth as the one on the Mississippi. One of the ropes, guiding the ferry, broke, causing a delay until another could be attached. The efficiency of the ferry crew was an indication that the problem was a common one.

Only eight were on the coach, now. Five of the original nine had stayed in Fort Smith, including the obnoxious book 'drummer'.

After crossing into Indian Territory, the roads were some of the roughest they would experience. They wound thru the San Bois mountains, which were beautiful. At the Red Oak station, they had to wait for a wheel to be repaired. Due to shifting soil and erosion, there was a constant change in the rock roads and the rough creek crossings. Therefore, damaging a wheel in this area was common.

This station was larger than most. The station agent's home, and the room which served as the ticket office, were on one side. Five guest rooms were on the other side, with a covered breezeway (better known as a 'dog-trot') between the two buildings. The, spring fed, Brazile creek was close to the station. Most of the passengers took advantage of the shallow water, to cool their feet for a while.

When the trip resumed, the station agent, Mr. Hardaway, was on board. He was going ride to McAlester, to replace the parts he'd used on the damaged wheel. Mr. Hardaway was a Choctaw Indian. He explained the territory they were traversing, and told the story about the Choctaw People being moved from their homelands, in Mississippi, to their new home in Oklahoma, Indian Territory. Because it was a very interesting story, with some sad parts, it made the trip go a little faster. He also told them that the stage would remain in Choctaw lands, after the trip resumed southward, until they passed Durant Station. They would cross the edge of the Chickasaw Nation for about two hours, before reaching Colbert's Ferry, on the Red River.

Three days after leaving Fort Smith, and crossing the Arkansas River, the troupe was ready to cross the third major river, Red River. This meant leaving Indian Territory and entering the State of Texas. Because of the delay, when repairing the coach's wheel, they missed the exchange with the east bound Concord. There would be an overnight stay at Colbert's Ferry. The next stage would arrive there at three p.m. the next afternoon, which was on a Sunday.

Captain Davis Jackson asked the station attendant if there was a church near, and was told "Yes sir, Cap'n, jist one block down th' street on th' left. Ya cain't miss it."

The station had a building very similar to the Red Oak station, but had six guest rooms. All three women were assigned individual rooms, three men had individual rooms, but two of the men didn't want to stay at the station.

The local 'hotel/bar/brothel' was where they wanted to stay. All six, who stayed at the station, went to church services the next morning.

Dave, being attracted to Robin, decided not to miss a chance to be close to her. He squeezed into the pew beside her and the two of them shared a songbook. After the services, he offered to buy her dinner. *('Dinner' was the word most commonly used for the noon meal. 'Supper' for the evening meal.)* There was still plenty of time, before the coach arrived, and there wouldn't be a supper stop, since they'd be leaving late.

"Thank you, Captain, I'd be honored to join you." she replied. "However, I'm not sure what kind of eating establishments are in this 'lovely' town." The comment had a touch of sarcasm in it, considering the whole town was three blocks long, and half the businesses were considered 'disreputable'. The reverend recommended 'Macie's Diner', and the young couple were very pleased with the chicken 'n dumplings, corn on the cob, fresh spinach (seasoned with cured fat back) and Macie's delicious dried apricot pie.

"Thank you, Dave, that was a wonderful dinner. I'm so full now, I'll probably get seasick when we cross the river." Robin said, flashing a smile.

"Well", Davis replied, "With your permission, I *was* planning to sit next to you when we leave. But, if you're going to get sick on me, maybe I'd better sit on the rear seat, instead."

"OK," Robin said, "I won't get sick. I'd like it, if you'd sit beside me. In fact, I still haven't had the experience of sitting on the back seat, yet. You want to sit there?"

The stagecoach left the ferry, on the Texas side, at 5:15 p.m. The sun was already getting lower, but as the route made it's westward turn, sunlight still filled the coach. "The conductor told me that, after the second way station, we'd be traveling six hours until the next one." Davis told Robin. "That will be a good time to get a nap. He said the stops were farther apart in Texas, and most of the roads are good and smooth, as long as we don't hit any heavy rain."

The two of them were alone in the rear seat, now, with three passengers in each of the front two seats.

"At least we have a little more room to stretch, than the others do, Dave." Robin whispered. It was at that point, it dawned on her that, the young handsome man wasn't sitting next to his window. He was, actually, very close.

He leaned back toward her and whispered back, "Feel free to lay your head over here," he patted his shoulder, "Maybe you won't snore quite so loud."

She elbowed him in the ribs, and took his hand, laid her head on his shoulder and said, "Wake me up in San Francisco."

"Good Lord, man!" one of the passengers exclaimed, ten minutes later, "Someone tell the driver to stop this wagon! This drunk son-of-a-bitch just puked on the rest of us, up here." The driver pulled to a stop, helped the sick man out of the coach and onto the top, where he laid down.

"Sorry, folks. We'll be stoppin' at Preston, soon and we'll give y'all time to clean up, if you'll do it quick. This crap happens pretty reg'lar, when these some of these fellers spend the night, in places like Colbert's Ferry has. The agent at Preston's got the stuff to clean the coach out with. Now we gotta get movin'. Th' sick'un kin spend th' night on top. He'll be okay by mornin'.'"

The damage wasn't quite as bad as the first man had complained about. Evidently the man had emptied out before boarding that morning. Only two people got vomit on their shoes. It wasn't long before the trip resumed, and wound west, during the night, through the northern part of Texas, to Jacksboro, where the route turned southwest.

Notable places such as Fort Belknap, Fort Phantom Hill and Abilene, fell behind them as the trip went smoothly through the first half of the 'Lone Star' state. There had been one spot, north of Abilene, where the rain cooled things off for a while. It was a welcome change from the increasingly higher temperatures.

The driver told the passengers that he was glad it didn't rain hard, or the mud could have caused as much as two or three days delay. Four days after crossing the Red River, they arrived at Fort Chadbourne, the next major landmark on the journey.

Robin and Davis had remained in the rear of the coach for that entire leg of the trip. They talked about their younger years, and their plans for the future.

Davis was the third of four sons. He grew up in Tennessee, the son of a soldier. He went to West Point Military Academy, and had been in the Army for eleven years. He was twenty seven years old, and had recently become very infatuated with an nineteen year old lady from West Virginia.

He was also re-thinking his decision to re-enlist, for another five years.

The fact was, for the last few days, he and Robin held hands nearly all the time. During the night time hours, he would kiss Robin's cheek, or forehead, while she was sleeping. What he didn't know was, that she did the same to him.

On the last night, before reaching Fort Chadbourne, she kissed his cheek, thinking he was asleep. When his eyes opened, she smiled. He reached up, pulled her lips to his, and they kissed long and deeply. Both, then, slept soundly.

Fort Chadbourne was a sizeable post, with it's own dry goods store, hardware store, two boarding houses, a telegraph office, and the largest livery that Davis Jackson had seen, except for the one at West Point. There was also a saloon, and enough barracks for more than 400 soldiers. He was offered the use of a vacant cabin, in the area of the officers' quarters.

Davis told Robin to go inside, bathe, and get some rest. There would be only a two and one-half hour stop, and he had other matters which needed tending, after which he would get a quick bath.

While Robin napped, Davis wired The Presidio, in San Francisco, where he was being re-assigned for the remainder of his tour of duty. The wire read, *'to Col. Abrams. Stop. Arrived Ft. Chad. Stop. Resume travel today. Stop. Arrive S.F. twelve days. Stop. Subject en route same coach. Stop. Will post again Ft. Yuma. Stop. Capt. D. Jackson.'*

After sending the wire, he reported to the post commander, as his orders specified.

He reported that there were two passengers, other than he and Robin, who had been on the full trip, since it departed Memphis.

One was an older woman, Maria Pelton. In her thirties, she was a very attractive woman, and had been the object of close inspection, by some of the men passengers.

The other was a tall man, Joseph Hawkins, in his forties. The man was well dressed, and could be easily taken as a rancher. He wore expensive boots, and a very nice western hat, made of brown beaver felt. He started the trip with a brown leather jacket, but had moved it under the seat as the weather got warmer. He carried his brown leather satchel every where he went.

The only time Davis Jackson wasn't observing the man, was when the man was in the coach, asleep, or otherwise occupied. His main assignment was to make sure Mr. Hawkins continued his journey to San Francisco. The brown satchel contained information, very sensitive to the United State Department of the Interior.

His report to Colonel James completed, Davis returned to the cabin, sat on the side of the bed, and kissed Robin awake. "Wow!" she said as she stretched, "A girl could get used to that. You better be careful who you wake up like that. Someone might tie you up and take you home with them."

"Home to West Virginia?" he asked with a grin, "I'm not sure I'll ever go back that direction."

"Well, if you're tied up, and the girl's driving the team, you just might be going that direction, anyway." She put her arms around his neck, and kissed him. "I need to ask you something, Dave. Will I see you after we get to San Francisco? If not, I need to be preparing myself now. I like you a lot, ... I mean a lot."

It was Davis' turn to speak. "I'm going to tell you some things, Rob. You have to swear to me, you won't say a word to anyone.

"But first, I'm going to answer your question. Although I've only known you for eleven days, I've never felt as close to any woman, as I do to you. I could talk for an hour about how smart, kind, pretty you are, and how comfortable it is to be with you. I've never known anyone I feel I can trust, more than you." He hesitated for a few seconds, drew a deep breath, and continued. "I love you, Robin Hopkins, and when we get to San Francisco, I'll ask your father for your hand, if you'll marry me."

"I'm not sure I can wait twelve more days, Captain Dave, I wish we could get married right now! Oh, God, I love you, too." She kissed him, again and again.

"Now," Davis spoke as he was pushing her to arms' length, "You need to listen to me, and keep everything I say in total confidence. Mr. Hawkins and I are actually traveling together. He just doesn't know it. You know that bag he carries everywhere? He has information in it that belongs to the federal government, and I've been assigned to see that it arrives at the Presidio safely, and on time. There is a radical group of people, who could use the information in the bag, to cause major problems for the State of California. I'm not expecting to see anything happen, until we reach California, and hopefully, not then. I love you. I want to marry you, but, I have to keep focused on Hawkins, for now. As soon as this is all done, I'll make you 'Mrs. Jackson'."

The dust was thick and blotted out Fort Chadbourne within the first quarter of a mile, after leaving the compound. There was a full compliment of nine passengers, again, and all were wearing scarves or bandanas across their faces.

A six-horse hitch was now taking them westbound, toward New Mexico and Arizona Territories, with a dip southward, where they traversed the barren plain between the Concho and Pecos rivers. Landmarks such as Horsehead Crossing, (where the agent had supplied cups of fresh goat's milk with their meal) Pope's Camp, Delaware Spring and Hueco Tanks all fell behind during the next four and one-half days. They were making excellent time through west Texas.

The only problems encountered were dust, heat, and one way station that had no horses to exchange. Comanches had raided the station, the night before, and had stolen twelve head. It was a fairly common occurrence at these remote outposts, but the Butterfield line would replenish them, within a day. The current team was fed and watered, and continued the trip, at a slower pace, until the next stop.

At the Delaware Spring stop, the driver was accosted by two 'desperados', approximately six years of age. He was checking wheel hubs when he turned to face the bandits. "Whoa!" He was looking into the barrels of two wooden guns, one had been whittled from a board, the other was a crooked stick. As he threw up his hands, he asked, "What you two hombres wantin'?"

"We's wantin' all yer cash." came the reply, from a squeaky little voice. "Now ya git up there an' chunk it all down 'ere, 'fore we hafta shoot ya!"

"Sorry, fellers, we ain't carryin' any money on this here stage. If they *was* some, I'd shore throw it down fer ya. I shore ain't wantin' t' git shot."

Overhearing what was going on, Davis Jackson stepped up behind the 'outlaws', poked his index fingers in their backs, and yelled, "Drop those guns, men, I got'cha covered!" The 'guns' hit the dirt, and the boys started to run. "You boys stop and get back here," Davis called. As the youngsters came up to him, he told them they could retrieve their 'weapons', but to stick them in their belts. He explained to them that he was an army captain and asked if they wanted to be soldiers. They looked at each other and nodded.

"Fine," Davis told them, "I need two good men here to keep an eye out for Indians, have you seen any?" Wordless, they shook their heads. "Well if you do see any, I need you to tell the station agent, right away."

"He's our paw!" You could hear the pride in the little guy's voice. "We'll tell 'im, soon's we see injuns."

"Good men," Davis responded, "Here's your army pay, and don't you be robbing any more stagecoaches." He handed them each a nickel. With big smiles, a 'wow!' and a, 'yeah, wow!', they headed for the trading post.

"People jist don' re'lize whut kinda dangers us Butterfield men hafta face, out here in Texas." The driver laughed. "It makes a body kinda nervous ta look down the barrel of a cupple o' guns. Thanks fer rescuin' me cap'n, now we got ta git. Ev'body load up, we's movin out!"

A cool, welcome breeze was coming off the mountains, when they arrived at Franklin, just north of El Paso, Texas. For three of the passengers, this was their last stop. The stage stop, here, had two bathhouses. The four lady passengers used one. The men passengers, drivers, and conductors used the other.

Due to a shortage of personnel on this part of the route, their driver and the conductor, for the trip to Tucson, would be exchanging places, occasionally, for the full stretch. It would be a tiring 360 miles, but with the smooth trail, and cooler than usual temperatures, they would make up a full day on their schedule.

With no more delays, it would still be ten more days to San Francisco.

The coach was lighter, now, with only seven occupants. Davis Jackson told the old, mustached, conductor that he was quite capable of handling a six-horse team, and would be glad to relieve either, or both of them, if needed. "Tell ya whut," the grizzled old veteran said, "We kin han'l th' drivin. Ya might spell us at shotgun, though." He jabbed his thumb toward the door of the stagecoach and added, "It's easier t' ketch a few winks inside thar, then up top."

There must have been fifteen stops, for mail and team changes. Personal needs had to be taken care of during those stops. Bagged breakfasts and lunches were supplied twice a day. Davis spent half the trip, in rotations, as shotgun rider, and thoroughly enjoyed being in Robin's arms, when it was his turn to rest.

"They wuz a time, when th' gals would hug me like thet." the conductor told Davis. "Course thet was a long time 'go. I was quite th' ladies man, in mah time. Why once't, I 'member, theys near 'bout sixty wimmin at a picnic. They was gonna auction off them box lunches, whut the wimmin brung. I didn' even know it, but them gals had a auction of they own, t' decide which one got ta share they lunch with me.

"Ophelia Jones won th' bid. Lawdy, she wuz the biggest, an' ugliest o' th' bunch. I thank some o' them others jist quit biddin', t' keep her from jumpin' on 'em. Anyways, thet wuz the bes' damn box full o' food I ever et. 'Fore th' day wuz over, her daddy wuz lookin' fer me, with a shotgun, if'n ya know whut I mean. I hauled my young ass outta Mizzou' an' ain't never been back. I heered later, thet she had twins. Both of 'em wus born'd with heavy mush-tasshes, ... jist like they maw's!." The old timer cackled and Davis laughed with him.

Now, they were on the last ten miles before Tucson. The last way station was in sight, and the regular driver would take over there. A five hour stop at Tucson would give everybody a much needed rest, time to clean up, and an opportunity to find a good, filling meal.

Davis wired to the Presidio. He gave their whereabouts, and proposed schedule for the rest of the journey. He reported that Mr. Hawkins was fine and still in possession of the documents. He was instructed, by return wire, that there were new orders awaiting him when he reached the post.

The Sonoran Desert was the next hurdle for those six travelers, which continued on, toward Fort Yuma. There had been a rare rain shower about half way through that stage of the journey. "When there is an appreciable rain on the desert," Davis offered, "The plants take full advantage of it. Look at all the blooms on the cactus plants." He looked at Robin and grinned, "I've been told it's some of the richest . . . Ouch!"

Her elbow had reached it's mark, again. Hawkins and Miss Pelton smiled, at each other. Having traveled with the young couple from the start of the journey, they, of course, were fully aware of the reason for Robin's punch. "Good shot, Miss Hopkins," It was only the second time Mr. Hawkins had spoken to her, since the beginning, "It would take a lot more than water to make this God forsaken desert rich for farming."

This section of the trip went a little slower. The company was still using six horses on this stretch, but were traveling slower. There was a way station everywhere water could be found. Hand dug wells provided the water needed for the station agents, and livestock. Since all the water was pulled up by hand, not a drop was wasted. Even bath water was poured into a 'sluice' type filter, which removed the dirt and soap, thru sand filled trays. The filtered water was then used to clean the draft horses, and coaches.

At one of these stops, Davis Jackson and another passenger, who was on his way to Los Angeles to help design and build a new water treatment system, were intrigued by the process. "I even drink this water," the station agent told them. "We won't give it to any other folks, but it's as clean as the water which comes from the well."

Davis was thinking how a similar system could be utilized at military posts.

About two miles after leaving that stop, it suddenly got darker and it started to rain hard. "How about this?" Joseph Hawkins spoke up, "It's a rare occasion that it rains like this, in this part of Arizona. It probably feels pretty cool on the men up top."

Five minutes later, the rain stopped. Only a couple of minutes after that, the coach lurched and jerked to a stop, with the driver yelling at his team "Skeedaddle, ya damn, worthless pieces o' buzzerd bait! Ya cain't be tuckerd out!"

The stage was stuck.

The conductor, soaked to the skin, climbed down and told the riders, they'd have to get out, to lighten the load. The mud was only four or five inches deep on each side of the coach. But the left set of wheels were sunk to the axle, in a track. "I should'a pulled her over a little outten the wore out tracks." the driver explained, "I guess th' water settled in thet deep part, an' made it softer. Well, all ya men git in back n' help push this thang out."

One of the men grumbled a little, but got behind the rear boot and pushed. After a few minutes, no progress was made.

Robin, and the other women, trudged to the back of the coach and put their shoulders into it, too. "Well, it looks like we have to come up with another plan." she said after still not moving the Celerity, which was the lighter style of coach.

One of the passengers, who appeared to be Indian, spoke, "I walk to station, get help." Without hesitating, he removed the shoes from his sun-browned feet, and left at a trot, removing his shirt as he was running back down the trail.

"Damn," the driver said, "didn' take long fer him to make up his mind." I was fixin' ta head back thet d'rection, myself. I weren't gonna be movin' thet fast, though."

The Indian, along with the station agent, and a team of mules, were back in about an hour. The process of hitching the mules to the other team, and pulling the coach out of the hole, was a quick one. Robin had walked down the road, and retrieved the Indian's shirt and shoes. She pulled them from the boot, and handed them to him. "Thank you, sir. It was very kind of you to do this for us. May I ask your name?"

He simply answered "I Chi-ka-na".

"Well then, thank you Mr. Chi-ka-na." she replied, inclining her head.

"Not 'meester', just Chi-ka-na." was his response.

"Nuff chit-chat, now, the driver called, you ladies git th' mud offen yer skirts, men kick it offen yer boots, 'n let's git rollin'."

The coach pulled into Yuma, Arizona at 6:30 a.m. on June first. Twenty-five minutes later, their ferry docked on the California side of the Colorado River. Several soldiers were on hand when the Celerity braked to a stop, in front of the Butterfield office. Davis was the first out his side of the coach, and helped the ladies out. He had noticed that Joseph Hawkins was still asleep, as they had driven thru the post gates. When Hawkins didn't get off the coach, Davis reached in and shook him.

Hawkins fell forward, dead. Davis looked quickly at the passengers, who were heading for the next coach. Maria Pelton had left the group and was walking toward a small buggy. Joseph Hawkins' brown leather satchel was in her hand. She had been sitting next to Hawkins during the night.

"Stop that buggy!" Davis yelled at the troopers. Just as Maria Pelton jumped into the rig, one of the soldiers threw his hands up to grab the reins at the horse's head. The horse shied.

The man driving the buggy, touched the whip to the horse's rump and wheeled the rig around, heading toward the gate, with Davis Jackson directly in his path.

Davis drew his pistol, yelled for the man to stop, and pulled the trigger. The .44 slug hit the horse in the head, causing it to tumble to the right, and twisting the buggy to an angle that caused both occupants to be thrown from their seats.

The buggy driver came to his feet and pulled a gun from his belt. As he brought it up toward Davis, the army captain cocked his Colt Dragoon, again, squeezed the trigger, and sent the man to the depths of hell.

Armed soldiers started calling for Davis to drop his gun. He calmly holstered it, removed his identification papers from his shirt pocket and told a corporal. "My name is Captain Davis Jackson. Detain that woman immediately. She's to be charged with murder. I'll explain the details, later. Get me that brown bag, and escort me to your commanding officer. Now, soldier! And hold that coach. It's going nowhere until I say so".

Two hours later, with a four-mule hitch, the troupe was in route west, again, carrying nine passengers. They would go as far as San Diego, then turn northward, at last.

The post commander at Fort Yuma agreed to take care of Joseph Hawkins' body, in accordance with instructions from the Department of the Interior. A knife was found on Maria Pelton, who had Hawkins' blood on her hands and clothes. The woman would be charged with murder of a United States Government envoy. The death penalty would be requested.

Lieutenant Raymond Cross was quickly dressed in civilian clothes, and ordered to accompany Captain Jackson to the Presidio. Before leaving Fort Yuma, Davis had introduced him to Robin, and briefed him on their relationship. "Thank you for the information, sir," the lieutenant said, smiling, "I'll take good care of you and your lady."

Accompanying the troupe on this section was a U.S. Marshal and his prisoner. Robin and Davis relinquished their position, on the rear seat, to them. The man had been caught shooting whores, in a brothel in Yuma, Arizona. "He wasn't satisfied with what he got. Says he paid for more, . . . sorry, ladies." he apologized, for talking about a subject that was sensitive to many women. "He killed six of those poor girls and hurt another one, before the bartender caught him in the back of the head with an axe handle. Since it happened in one of the territories, I've got to take him to San Diego, to be tried in federal court. He'll hang for it."

Davis received one more elbow to the ribs, while they were passing the rich and fertile fields of southern California. "You're just not going to learn, are you?" Robin asked him.

"Actually, this is one of the places I know about, not just what someone told me." He smiled at Robin and continued, "We may settle down here, someday. Just look at the grape crops. One thing I learned in Tennessee was how to make excellent wine."

In Los Angeles, there was a seven hour lay-over. Again, while Davis was sending wires and checking other military business, Robin bathed, napped, then sent a wire, herself, to her father. *'Mr, Rupert Hopkins, c/o Virginia Rose Mine. Stop. Am in Los Angeles. Stop. See you in five days. Stop. Rob.'*

Lieutenant Cross joined Robin and Davis for supper. The Chinese laundry, three doors down from the stage office, had cleaned and pressed all their clothes, including the officers' dress uniforms. "I'll want to meet your father as soon as I can get away from the fort," Davis told her. "maybe it won't take long. I wired The Bay House for a room reservation, and it will be waiting for you. I'll be there as soon as can. Do you know where you'll be meeting your father?"

"Why yes, Captain Jackson, as a matter of fact, I do." She was playing, now. "My father also has a room for me at, where else? The Bay House. Or maybe it's a suite of rooms, I can't remember. Maybe he owns the whole hotel. Who knows? He being a big, rich, mining tycoon, like he is. Ouch! Why did you elbow *me* in the ribs?"

Davis simply said, "You had one coming, or is it three or four?"

Robin's father was at the Butterfield 'terminal', as they liked to call the very last stop on the long trip. She introduced Davis and Raymond quickly, but they had an escort waiting.

"I'll see you later," he said, then gave her a quick kiss and told her father to "look after her until I get back." The men mounted and left at a trot.

"There must be something going on that I don't know about, young lady." her father spoke with his familiar, raspy voice, which she hadn't heard in over two years.

"Yes, Pop, you just met the man who will be your son-in-law, soon. You'll like him, Pop, you'll really like him. I love him more than anything. He's a wonderful human being. He's smart, confident, brave, ..."

"Whoa, Rob, wind down a little. I think I get the picture . . . . In fact, it sounds kinda like the way I felt about your mother, God rest her soul." Pop Hopkins looked into his daughter's eyes. "If he makes you happy, and never does anything to hurt you, then I'll be pleased to call him my son."

The two of them sat on the bench, in front of the hotel, and talked for a long time.

Davis rode up to the Bay House just before five. There was still an hour and a half of daylight left. As he went inside, he spotted Robin and Rupert in the dining room. When he walked up to their table, her father looked him over and turned to his daughter, "I thought you said this young man was a captain, Rob. I see he's wearing silver leaves on his shoulders."

Robin didn't know what he meant, referring to the 'silver leaves', and sat with a questioning look on her face.

"You're both right. Things have been happening fast. I was a captain. When I reached the Presidio, Colonel Abrams had already received orders to promote me to Major. That was, actually, effective two days after we left Memphis, Rob. Yesterday morning, *he* received a promotion, to brigadier general. He left the post, right after I arrived, taking the documents we brought, to Sacramento. He will be staying there and, since I was *now* the ranking officer, I became post commander. That automatically carries a minimum rank of lieutenant colonel." He smiled at Robin, bent and gave her a quick kiss, and asked her father, "May I join you, Mr. Hopkins?"

"No, no, son, call me "Pop.""

EPILOGUE

The most famous stagecoach line, in the history of our country, lasted only a short twelve years. The completion of the Transcontinental Railroad made 'the long trip' unnecessary. Many shorter stage lines were formed to haul passengers, and mail to railheads. During the Civil War, the Confederacy confiscated the majority of all coaches operating in their territory.

Robin Elaine Hopkins was married to Lt. Colonel Davis Jackson on June fifteenth.

Newly appointed Captain, Raymond Cross, served as best man.

Military obligations kept the newly weds from taking a honeymoon, so they stayed five days at The Bay House, which, incidentally, *was* owned by Rupert 'Pop' Hopkins. The hard working gold miner had hit a big load, and was now the sole owner of the Virginia Rose Mine, which he named after Robin's mother, Virginia, and her recently deceased step-mother, Rose. He had, also, become the owner of six other businesses in San Francisco.

Maria Pelton, a Mexican citizen whose real name was Maria Sandoval Ramirez, was convicted and hanged, at Fort Yuma, for the murder of U.S. federal envoy, Joseph Hawkins.

Quick action by the California State Congress, avoided a Mexican takeover of the southern half of the state. The copies of Spanish land grants, which were in the brown satchel, were instrumental in the development and passing of that legislation.

Robert 'Bob' Hopkins, Robin's twin brother, sold the dairy in West Virginia, and brought his wife to San Francisco, where he helped with the family businesses.

Fifteen years later, the wines of Jackson Vineyards were judged the finest in California.

'Bitch'

It must have been 115 degrees in the northern part of Arizona territory. I guess it was still Arizona, it may have been the top floor of hell, for all I knew. The bugs, which sometimes came in swarms, all wanted to share in the feast that my face provided. My clothes, boots and gloves protected the rest of my lean, and stinky body, but for my horse, there was no sanctuary. Her tail was so worn out from swatting at flies, that she was using all it's length to just keep them off her ass.

I felt an unusually painful sting and, as I reached to shoo the damn critter from my neck, I heard the crack of a long rifle.

Immediately, I left the saddle and hit the desert floor, rolling. Just as I came to rest behind a prickly pear cactus, one big leaf shattered and sprayed aloe vera all over my face, along with some of the barbed needles. Another shot! Aloe vera may be fine for burns and such, but *it* does the burning when it gets in the eyes.

Lying flat, I was out of sight, as much as I could be. I realized, then, that the sting I'd felt earlier was actually the first bullet, nicking my neck. I decided to lie as still as I could. My eyes quit burning within a few minutes, but those needles were hurting my face.

Maybe the Jones boys would think they finally took me out, with that last shot. If so, they would either move on, or come from hiding to make sure their job was finished. Either way, I was in a predicament. My neck was bleeding, drawing more of those damn biting flies. I had cactus needles in my face. I couldn't see where my horse had gone, or if it was wounded, too.

I guess the thing I was most upset about, was the fact that, I had let them discover where I was. The oppressive heat had caused me to not be as alert as I should have been. I had closed my eyes, for a few minutes, several

30

times. It doesn't take much to catch a man off guard, in that desolate, wide open, God-forsaken country. Six long days in my worn out saddle had taken the edge off my senses, which are usually as sharp as anyone's.

It was still three or four hours till sundown, at which time the temperature would drop quickly. My only choice was to lie there and wait. Patience never was one of my strong points, either.

I noticed a slight depression in the sand to my left, and started inching toward it very slowly. One of the problems, in that part of the country, is . . . . *rattlesnakes like depressions in the sand.* However, after several minutes of slow movement, I was close enough to tell there were none there. I had heard stories about the Apaches, and how they would bury themselves in the sand, which would then reflect the heat from the sun.

It was told that Geronimo had pulled this, more than once, on army patrols. It's said that he would rise up from the sand behind the last soldier, and sit, watching them ride into the distance. General Crook, himself, stated that Geronimo was the smartest strategist he ever encountered.

I moved my hands and feet slowly & cautiously until I was able to cover my old, worn out (and second hand), blue uniform pants and my green plaid shirt. If the Jones' came looking for me, at least they would have to get close, before spotting me. I knew my sun-browned face would blend with the sand, so I left much of it uncovered. My hat was lying on the ground, where it landed after I left my horse.

Nothing moved, anywhere. Dark finally came, and with it a rapid cool-down. It was so dark, I was afraid to move around much, until the stars lightened the sky some. The moon wouldn't rise for a while, yet, so I just eased back to where my hat was resting, collected it, and started squinting my eyes for any sign of my horse.

She wasn't a comfortable riding horse. Nor did she look good or move fast. But, she was seven years old, durable, and never cantankerous, like some I'd owned. I guess I could have given her a nicer name, but at the time, "Bitch" just seemed appropriate for the gal that was going to have to spend a lot of time with me.

As the moon started coming up, I saw a faint light, probably two miles away. The desert can play tricks on you, but it was the only thing I'd seen to give me hope of any kind. As I headed toward what must have been a campfire, I decided that the Jones boys would never see another sunrise, if it was, indeed, their camp.

Another hour later, I was within a few yards of the dying campfire. With only one horse, and one lone figure in sight, I sat on my heels for a while before deciding to approach. I laid flat on the ground, but before calling out, I saw movement on the other side of the fire, and eased my .45 from my holster. The man, at the campfire, pulled iron, too, indicating that he wasn't expecting company.

I was relieved when I saw it was ol' Bitch, ambling toward the camp. As she angled toward the other horse, the man moved away from the light of the campfire. I figured it was in order to watch for any other company, which may come in from the dark.

I decided to keep quiet for a while, and watch for any other activity myself. If the Jones boys were trying to slip up on the stranger's camp, I would be more help if they thought this guy was alone.

After a few minutes, I caught a glimpse of movement to my right. It was the camper, making a slow round, circling his camp. He passed within ten feet of where I lay still, and cautiously moved on. I would guess that an hour had passed, since Bitch had walked into camp. Then the man came out of the shadows and moved directly to the horses. He inspected Bitch carefully, hobbled her, and found some grain for her in a sack, near the fire.

He then watered both horses from a water bag, refilled his cup with coffee, and sat back on the ground, just out of the brightest light.

Since I was feeling comfortable with the survey taken by the man in camp, I decided it was time to make my presence known. I holstered my Smith & Wesson, which I had still been holding. But, again, before I called out to camp, the man raised up, unbuckled his gunbelt, then the one holding his pants up. It was time to relieve himself of the coffee he'd been drinking. He took a few steps back, but to my surprise, he dropped his drawers, squatted, and let loose a stream.

Shit! He was a woman.

After gathering my thoughts, I remembered how quickly this lady cowboy had drawn her gun, and how patiently she scouted the surrounding area. She was no greenhorn. I decided to wait a while longer, so she wouldn't think I'd found out her secret.

I waited about another hour, and as she started to make out her bedroll, I called out, but not too loudly. She drew her pistol, stepped farther away from the fire light, and called back for me to come on in, empty handed.

"No problem" I told her. "I lost my horse, saw the light from your fire, and was hopin' she had found it, too. Looks like I was right."

As I walked closer, I could see she had her hand gun trained on my mid-section. "No need to point that thang at me, mister, I'm so damn tired, my butt won't be draggin' in here for 'nuther hour or two." I said. "She threw me about mid-day, and I been walking ever since. That coffee smells purty good, mind if I have some?"

She told me that she only one cup, and wasn't fond of sharing it with someone she didn't know. I told her that the bay horse was the one I'd lost, and I had a cup in my pack, if she'd let me get it. Under the point of her gun & watchful eyes, she allowed me to open my roll & retrieve my cup.

I looked over my mount, and she seemed to be ok. No wounds, that I could see in the dim light, just tired, like me. I patted her on the muzzle, and told her "You're a good girl, Bitch."

"What did you say?" asked the gun toting woman, as she lifted the weapon towards me. I quickly explained that the horse's name was Bitch, and I would never call a man, with a gun, a bitch. "You don't need to be calling a bitch, with a gun, a man, either." There, she had told me the truth, she was a woman. So at least, she was being honest with me. She was still holding the gun on me, so I decided to wait, before telling her I had already figured it out.

She asked who I was & why I was in these parts. I explained that I was trailing some men who had killed my 15 year old brother, raped their own sister, and left her for dead, intending to blame the rape on my brother. They claimed they caught him in the act of killing her, and they cut his throat, to teach him a lesson. The Jones boys weren't very smart.

After they brought their sister's body home, she awoke long enough to tell her parents that her own two brothers were the ones who assaulted her, *after* killing my brother.

"I've been huntin them no-goods for purt-near three years, and I catched up with 'em once't. I shoulda jist killed 'em on the spot, but 'stead, I took 'em to the laws in Fort Worth Texas, where they 'scaped." I explained.

I noticed my host was lowering her pistol, a single action Colt Navy, and felt a little more at ease.

"How 'bout you, lady? Whut you doin way out here all alone?"

"I'm looking for two men, go by the last name of Jones. They stole four good horses from my ranch last week. Three of my best mares and the best stud I've ever owned. When I find them, I'll kill them."

From the tone of her voice, and the way she handled her gun, I knew she would do just that.

"Was it Bud and Jack Jones?' I asked. When she told me yes, I explained to her that it was the same ones I was after. She seemed more relaxed after that, and told me to get my bedroll. It was getting late, and morning was going to come at the same early time, tomorrow. Then she said, "By the way, I sleep alone, except for my .44. It's all the company I need, understand?"

"Don't worry, ma'm, I'm not anywheres like them Joneses. You kin rest without worrying yourself about me." It only took me a few minutes to strip the saddle from Bitch, make out my bedroll, and get comfortable. The woman must have been really tired, she was already snoring, mildly, before I closed my eyes.

I was up, had stirred up the campfire, made a pot of coffee, and gone away from camp to 'take a leak', when I heard her clearing her throat and yawning. I called to her that I would be back in a minute, and she should have a cup of coffee. Both cups were full when I walked back to the fire, but she had gone the other direction from camp, in order to relieve her own self.

When the woman returned, I said, "You know, I didn't 'member to intro-duce m'self last night. I'm Hank. Hank Hawkins. I'm 'riginally from east Texas, pert-close to Jefferson. My folks got a farm there, but they prob'ly sold it, by now and moved to town. Me and Ted, my li'l brother, was the only hep my folks had. Ma sews a lot fer other ladies, and pa, he's a good blacksmith, so I 'magine they's moved."

The woman introduced herself as Esmirelda Higgins. "If you ever call me by that name, I'll shoot the heels off your boots. Everybody calls me 'Ellie'." She and her husband owned a horse ranch, in a large valley, north of Cuba, in New Mexico Territory. She said that her husband had died nearly a year ago, in an accident, while rounding up wild mustangs.

Ellie had run the ranch alone since, with the help of a foreman and two other hands. The Jones boys had shown up a little over two weeks before, and Ellie had hired them to help with fence building. Most of her ranch was open range, but when she and Matt, her husband, had bought the place, they decided to fence off four pastures, 100 acres each, in order to do some selective breeding and keep the pregnant mares away from over-active studs.

After a few days on the ranch, the Jones boys took the horses from one of the fenced pastures, at night time, and left, heading west. Ellie had followed them, as best she could, but had lost their trail yesterday.

I told her that I had heard talk, in Flagstaff, that they were headed to Colorado Springs. That was about a month ago, and I had no idea they had gone as far east as Cuba. Now they were closer than I thought, and must have spotted me in that little town, two days back. Knowing I was that close, they were probably waiting to bushwhack me, yesterday . . . . Maybe again today.

Ellie asked what was wrong with my face, and I remembered the cactus thorns. There were seven red, swollen places. Ellie told me she could help get them out, and pulled a large bowie knife from her belt. She scraped, backwards, slowly with the sharp edge of the knife blade, nicking the skin each time a needle came out.

I was not comfortable being this close to a woman, who had a sharp knife in her hand. I guess Ellie noticed me watching her 'assets' in her shirt. She drew the knife downward, then pulled the backside of it across my throat, slowly.

"What are you looking at?" she asked. I quickly closed my eyes and said "nuthin."

"Nothing? . . . . Are you saying I have nothing in my shirt?" the knife was now trailing up & down my cheeks and ears.

I was dumbfounded. I couldn't decide whether to say yes, or no. As I peeked thru one of my eyelids, I could see she was grinning. This woman was picking on me. I hardly even knew her, and she was teasing me with a bowie knife. . . . . and her breasts. "Ma'm," I said as she touched the point of the blade to the tip of my nose, "I mean no offense, but they's plenty in yore shirt, an' I'm a man. I cain't hep but look, if'n it's right in front of my face. That don't mean I'll be dis'spekful to you. I ain't thet kinda man."

Ellie stood up straight, slid her knife into it's scabbard, smiled and said, "I trust you, for now, Hank Hawkins, just don't do anything to change my mind."

We had some breakfast, beans and bacon, and discussed going after the Jones boys. Ellie wanted to hit the trail as fast as we could, in order to catch up with them, since they were probably not far ahead of us. I reminded her of the excellent mounts they had stolen, and that we'd have a hard time catching them, on a straight run. I was sure it was them that shot at me yesterday.

I told her I was a damn good tracker and I'd take the point, ride a wide circle ahead, and try to locate them. She said that she was going with me, that two pairs of eyes were better than one. I disagreed, but not to her face.

As I started to saddle my horse, I decided to do a little teasing, myself. "Git over here, Bitch, an' you better behave yerself, too."

"What did you say?" Ellie called out.

"Oh, . . . sorry 'bout thet one, guess I'm gonna have to change this ol' hoss's name".

We were a little later breaking camp than we should have been, but we found a wide, clear arroyo and rode in it for miles. There were a few small water holes in it, so water was no problem. Around mid-day, we broke from the old river bed, and headed for a rare tree line. Trees in this country usually indicated water . . . . A river, large water hole or a spring trickling down a hillside.

I told Ellie to dismount, tie her horse to some scrub brush, and follow me, slow and low. A good campsite, with water, is good for all creatures, whether they have four legs or two. We eased up to the first trees, and started making our way thru the growth.

First, we spotted her horses. She tapped me on the shoulder, pointed at the horses, and silently mouthed the word, "mine".

The Jones boys must have thought they finished me, yesterday, and were sleeping late today. They didn't even know we were there, until we had our guns in their faces. We had silently removed theirs, from within their reach. I nudged Jack Jones in the ribs, with my foot. When he opened his eyes and mouth, I jammed my pistol across his tongue, and into his throat.

Ellie put her gun right next to Bud's ear and pulled the trigger. He jumped up, and stumbled over their wood pile. Before he even knew what was going on, Ellie shot again. This time it went into Bud's leg, and he went down yelling. We kept both guns on them, and I asked Jack which one of them had cut my brother's throat.

I pulled my pistol from his mouth, he coughed and answered, "Bud did it! Bud caught 'em kissin' an' jerked 'im up an' slit his throat!"

"You lyin' sonuvabich, Jack!" Bud yelled, "You wuz tryin' to git in Sally's pants, 'n you heered her telling' Will 'bout it. Will faced you 'n you knocked him down. Then you cut his throat, like'n he weren't nuthin but a hog. Then you jumped on Sally 'n took her first. Then, after I had her, you beat her 'til you thought she's daid".

I asked Ellie if I could borrow her knife. She handed it to me, I put it to Jack's neck, and said "You deserve worse'n this, Jack Jones, but now we' even." With all the strength I could muster, I sliced the blade halfway thru his neck, and watched him bleed to death, kicking in the Arizona sand.

"This one is mine" Ellie said as she holstered her gun. She threw Bud's gun to him & told him to reach for it. He didn't want to touch it, but it was his only chance to live. "You better pick it up, you damn horse thief," she told him. He grabbed for it, but just as his hand closed around the grip, two bullets ripped thru his head, blowing blood and brains all over the campfire.

"You wuz takin a chance let'n that sorry piece o' shit go for his gun". I said.

Ellie smiled, jacked out her spent shells, and said, "It wasn't loaded."

EPILOGUE

We stopped at the first town we came to, and told the local sheriff where he could find the Jones boys' bodies. We kept their saddles, guns, knives and money. I wired home, to East Texas, sending word to my folks where I was, and what had happened.

For the next six days, I helped Ellie get her horses home. She offered me a job, and since I'd done nothing but hunt the Jones boys, for the last three years, I accepted.

A couple of days later, we had the stallion in the lot near the barn. As he was mounting a fine black mare, Ellie put her hand on my shoulder and said, "You know what, Hank? I think I'm ready for a little stud service, myself".

That was five years ago. Yesterday, we were at the same lot, watching our son riding his fine young pony. It balked, tossing him onto the ground. As it trotted to the far corner, he jumped up and yelled, "Git back here, Bitch!"

My wife chuckled, kissed me on the cheek, and said, "Like father, like son."

A Lawyer For 'Dirty' Allen

"At's a fine pelt yer woman's cleanin' dere, Lizard," John 'Dirty' Allen told his best friend, "One o' th' bes' I seen in a spell."

"Yip, it's a goodun, the big ol' booger didn't wanna go down easy, either. I kept thinkin' he was gonna git to me b'fore I could git back up." Jeremy Maurice Spencer, 'Lizard' as he was know in the mountains, was telling the story of the grizzly that almost killed him, yesterday. "I put six slugs in his big ol' chest, an' he jist kep on comin' at me. I hadn' stumbled on thet damn log, I'da jist jumped under 'im, stuck m' blade in his ass, an' ripped 'im up th' belly. Once't I got t' his heart, I'da jerked it out an' crammed down his throat. That's th' way I usually kill 'em."

"Why you ol' turd, I kinda wish he'd o' gone 'head an' cleaned yer ol' plow. Then I wouldn' hav' ta' lissen to yer crap."

One of the codes mountain men lived by, was to not call another mountain man a liar. You could tell him he's full of bull, crap, baloney, or any number of other objects. You could just flat disagree with him. The most effective way of indicating your doubt was, to just shake your head and walk away, laughing. Just do not call a man a liar. That would could get you killed. It was a way of life in the high country.

The man without a good tale had very few friends.

A man with a good tale was highly respected in their 'social circles', although 'respect' was not the word used when one man discussed another. 'He's alright' or 'He'll do' was about the closest thing to a compliment you'd find, but the insults and name calling were common practice.

Lizard had been in the mountains for over twenty years. He'd met Dirty at a rendezvous, down at Cripple Creek, eighteen years ago. They had been trading beaver pelts, in the post, when Lizard noticed the three young Indian women with Dirty. "Yip," Dirty said, "I give thet ol' 'rapaho chief a steel blade, an' a ol' sailor hat, thinkin' he mite 'preciate it by not eatin' my gizzerd, an' he wound up giv'n me three wimmen. I thank they was gittin' to ol' to marry, an' he jist wanted ta git rid of 'em. "Course they follers me 'round, like pups lookin' fer a hind tit. "Guy over yonder wanted to gimme some whisky fer the youngun, but I cain't han'l thet shit he dranks. 'Sides, she's th' onliest one I like. Th' others'll work they asses off, but Blue Bird's th' one what *won my li'l heart.*"

Lizard laughed and the two shared beer, at a table in the back of the post. After a couple rounds, Lizard noticed the oldest of the three girls, who was probably in her early twenties, watching every move he made. "Ya reckon thet girl in th' longest braids is flirtin' with me?" he asked, "She jist cain't seem ta take her big brown eyes offen me."

"Naw, she's jist per-tektin me." Dirty answered, "If I'ze ta git drunk, an' you'd try ta hurt me, er rob me, she'd cut yer throat with her skinnin' knife. Th' ol' thang's made o' black glass, they calls it o'sidjun, er sumthin like thet. It's 'bout eight eenches long. She kin skin a beaver with it 'n lesser'n three minutes. I kin shave with mah steel blade, but I cain't git it sharp as thet piece o' black glass."

"Mebbe I'll git me a woman like 'at, someday," Lizard commented. "I guess I needs me a woman. Need her fer more'n skinnin' beavers, too." He grinned at Dirty, then at Red Bird, the object of discussion. "Man's gotta thank 'bout his future. Y' ev'r tho't 'bout gettin' rid of th' extra gals?"

"Yip," Dirty replied, "'Fact is, Skinner O'Donnel wants ta trade me a big mule an' twenny beaver fer Yellow Bird, she's th' middle one. Thank I'll take 'im up on thet'un, too. Blue Bird takes care o' ever'thang I need. 'Fact, I ain't never had th' other two in th' sack. They's shore been fightin' over me, though, me havin' whut I got, ta please 'em with. Them two feel plumb mistreated, not gittin' ta use me. I kinda thank ol' Red Bird likes ya, Lizard. I'd make you a deal on 'er if yer in a mood fer a woman."

Lizard didn't sleep alone that night. The extra Sharps Big 50 was all he needed to swing the deal. He still had his own Sharps, and it didn't shoot to the left, like the trade gun. He also had accumulated two Henry long guns, and one of the new Henry repeating rifles. Two .44 caliber Navy Colts were always in his belt, and a .44 Colt Dragoon, he kept wrapped in oilcloth, was in his pack. Three knives were at his disposal, one in a scabbard just below the back of his neck. The others were inside each high-top moccasin. His most used weapons, though, were his ham-like fists. Without exception, all who had faced them had lost. At six feet, three inches tall, and three hundred pounds, Lizard Spencer was a menacing figure.

"You wouldn' be th' type man who'd blow a little smoke up 'nother man's backside, would ya now, Dirty?" Lizard asked the smaller man the next day. "Ol' Red Bird tol' me las' nite, thet I was lots better in th' sack then you is. Ya tol' me ya ain't never had her,"

"Well, Lizard, mebbe I did. Blue Bird tells me alla time, I fergits thangs. Guess I musta had her once't and jist fergot."

"At's awright, Dirty, you damn sure din't hurt her, *with whut you got.* Jist 'member, I bought her, fair and square. Ain't nobody else got any bizness messin' with her. Ya mite kinda spread thet word 'round. By the way, I seed Skinner leavin' a'while ago with th' middle sister. Guess ya made th' trade."

"Yip," he answered, "I kinda felt sorry fer poor ol' Yeller Bird, too. Th' sweet li'l thang was so bent outta shape over losin' me, I thought she'd cut her own throat. She wuz hangin' on t' my coat, an' crying her fool haid off, when Skinner dragged her off. *She jist loved me soooo bad.*"

"Yeah?" said Lizard, "She musta got over ya purty quick. When I seed her, she was smilin' big an' ridin' thet big black o' Skinner's. He wuz ridin' a big ol' mule." Lizard chuckled and added, "Guess she musta made a deal o' her own."

Lizard stopped, helped Red Bird turn the bear skin over, patted her on the butt, and walked on with his friend. "Ya know, pard, when I traded ya outta thet womam, I tho't all I'ze needin' was a bed warmer, an' someone ta hep me work these skins. But'cha know whut? I don' know whut I'd do iffen she weren't around. 'Sides thet, she's give me three strong sons. She wants a gal baby, but I reckon they ain't gonna be no more pups fer us. Yessir, I needs 'er more'n anythin' else I got. I guess thet's love. She thanks so, too."

"Shit, Lizard, I ain't never heered ya talk thet kinda crap, 'afore. Gimme a cupple minutes an' I'll write a *love* song fer ya ta' sing 'er. 'Er mebbe I kin find some parchmen' paper an' hep you write a pome, *a love pome.*" Dirty cackled and took two quick steps away, just in case Lizard decided to reach for him. "Now, ya big, stinkin elyfant, ya know how I feels 'bout my Blue Bird, all these years. Hell, she even sav'd my ol' ass from dyin' twice't. A man jist ain't gonna make it out here 'thout a good woman. Onliest thang is, we ain't never had eny young'uns."

A tall young man, over six feet tall, came trotting up. "Whoo'zis?" Dirty asked his friend.

"Uncle Dirty," the boy said, "You know who I am. I'm Billy."

"WOAH!" Dirty exclaimed, "ain't no way you kin be li'l Billy. Hell, Billy ain't but 'bout this high". He leveled his hand at his waist. "Yip, I 'member, . . . 'bout this high. Dickie 'n Hawk, they's even littler."

"Dick's even bigger than me, Uncle Dirty, and Night Hawk is nearly as big. I'm sixteen, now, and those two are almost fifteen. They'll be here in a few minutes. I'm betting Night Hawk will get here first. He's faster, but still not as fast as me. Dick's a little bigger than me, but I'm the strongest."

The two other boys ran into camp, and straight to Dirty, with greetings and hugs for him, then for their mother.

"Damn, Lizard, you shore throwed some big ol' pups." he chuckled, "Good thang they looks like they maw, though. I'd hate fer enythang to look like you. I saw the fleas is even stayin' on th' back o' yer haid, jist so they kin stay 'way from yer face."

"Yep, they's good boys, too, Dirty. They kin track a frog 'cross water, run a deer down on foot, and shoot th' nose offen a mouse at a hunnert yards. Hawk, he's hell with a blade. Nex' rendezvous, he's gittin' in th' throwin' contest. Better put yer money on 'im, Dirty, I ain't never seen enyone as good. Guess he gits it from 'is maw's people. 'Course, Red Bird's blood's in all three of 'em."

Dirty stayed with the Spencer family for a week. He was so impressed with the boys, that he hated to leave for home. Home was close to a hundred miles away, near Homer's Peak. He and Blue Bird had a large cabin in a deep valley. The range of mountains, on each side, protected their valley from the worst of winters, and the harshest summers. The grass was high and thick. The mustangs, Dirty raised, were strong and fast. He had no problem marketing them to military posts, and mountain men in need of a good mount.

Several times during the week, he had mentioned how badly he wished he and Blue Bird had children of their own. He had things to be done at home that required additional help, and he said that he always wanted to teach 'young'uns' the skills to survive in the unforgiving mountains. Blue Bird had always wanted a daughter, too, to teach her skinning, tanning, cooking, and sewing skills.

Lizard, Red Bird, and the boys had several conversations over those few days. Dick, the largest of the twins, asked if he could go home with Dirty, until the next rendezvous, which was about four months away, in September. The rest of the family agreed that it would be a good thing for Dick, Dirty, and Blue Bird. Dick, himself, asked Dirty about it.

"Whoa!" Dirty yelled, "Now why in hell'd I want t' have a big ol' brat like you follerin' me 'round? I'd hafta be pertectin' ya from injuns, lions, b'ars, 'n probly wimmin. Big as y' are, they's gonna thank yer old 'nuff to git hitched. Now, boy, d'ya still thank ya wantin' ter run these hills with this here ol' man?"

"I'm not really wanting to be with you all that much, Uncle Dirty." Dick grinned as he answered his uncle, "That's not my reason to go home with you. It's just been so long since I've seen my beautiful aunt Blue Bird. If it weren't for seeing her, I wouldn't even think of running these hills with your ugly old ass. In fact, I thought I'd just follow behind you, a mile or so, and hide if we meet anyone. Being seen with you might ruin my reputation."

"Ya little turd, yer jist like yer daddy, well, mayhap not quite as ugly." Dirty countered. "I guess ya kin go with me, but if'n ya git t' actin up, I'll send yer butt back home so fas', yer hair won' get home 'til two days later. 'Nother thang, if we's 'round other folk, don' call me 'uncle'. I ain't wantin' no one to know I'ze related to yer ugly carcass. An' git yer pack ready, I'ze leavin' at dawn."

Needless to say, it was an emotional parting the next morning. Red Bird cried, seeing Dick ride of with his uncle. She knew he was in good hands, but he was her favorite, not as aloof as his twin brother, Night Hawk, nor as boisterous as Billy. Dick was always the first to hug her, help her with her work, fetch things for her or stay with her when the others were hunting. She was going to miss him, badly.

The rider came up to Lizard's front door at a gallop. The horse had been ridden hard, and long. "Lizard! Lizard!" he called.

Hawk was the first one out the door, followed by Lizard and the others. It was nearly dark, and the dry mountain air was cooling rapidly.

"Mack Dawkins!" Lizard spoke, "Whut're ya doin' runnin' in here like thet? A man could git in t' lots o' trouble, ridin' up an yellin' like a drunk injun."

"Ya gotta hurry, Lizard. Yer boy's hurt bad, an' Dirty's in th' clink! I'ze not real shore whut happen', but Dirty tol' me t' git ya there, fast as ya could ride. They's in 'Lead Ears', thet French-Canuck town by th' old tradin' post, north o' here. Hurry, Lizard. If'n ya got a good fresh hoss I kin use, I'll ride with ya."

"Ya jist stay here fer a cupple days, Mack, ya kin keep Red Bird company 'til ya git rested." Lizard started giving orders, "Ya boys git three good hosses saddled. Red Bird, we'll need our blankets, an' guns. Git us plenty o' shells, we don' know how long it'll take, er whut we'z gittin' in th' middle of."

"I git guns an' shells. Tell boys saddle me hoss. I go. No talk." Red Bird made it plain to all what she was going to do. No one questioned her.

The boys saddled five of their best horses. Mack had made it clear that he didn't want to rest, and was going to return to Le Dereis with them.

Ten minutes after Mack had ridden in, the party was riding back out. Before he mounted up, Lizard went into the cabin, and returned with a hard, doe skin covered case. A knowing glance passed between the boys and their mother, but not a word was said.

Le Dereis was one of the older trading post towns in the Rockies. Many of the American trappers had trouble pronouncing the name, hence it became 'Lead Ears' to many. It was, also, the only post left in the area which traded, almost exclusively, with the French and Canadian trappers in the area. They were an unruly and selfish lot. The advance of American trappers, with moral codes and respect for the other man's territory, was contradictory to their own way of life. Because of that, and the lowest prices paid for pelts, most mountain men stayed away from Le Dereis.

The current post 'adjutant', as he liked to be called, was Fillipe Donielle Rene' Brisbois. He resented the fact that American trappers refused to trade with him. He had enlisted some of the worst of his French-Canadians to ruin, or rob, traplines belonging to the Americans. His theory was that, by harassing the Americans, they would be forced to leave the area, leaving more beaver and other game for his own trappers. He had decided that the town should be under his control, too, and had arranged for one of his own men, Lemuel Vines, to occupy the office of town marshal.

Lizard rode into town alone. His wife and sons had already slipped in, on side streets, and watched from different vantage points as he rode straight down the center of town. He walked his horse to the hitch rail in front of the small, log building marked 'JAIL'. As he walked through the door, the marshal stood up from his desk.

"Lizard!" Dirty yelled through the bars of the single, small cell, 'I'ze shore glad ya got here. They says I murdered some men, but I wuz jist gittin 'em offen Dickie. Do sumpin, Lizard."

"In a minute, Dirty," Lizard turned to the marshal and continued, "Where's my son?"

The marshal rested his right hand on the butt of his sidearm. "And who might you be?"

"I'll tell you three things, marshal," Lizard said, without a trace of the dialect used by mountain men all over the Rocky Mountains. "First, if you even act as though you're going to pull that gun, you'll be dead before you can clear your holster. Second, if any harm comes to my friend, here, you'll be dead before you can clear your holster. Third, if you don't tell me where my son is, NOW, I'll just kill you where you stand."

"He's across the street, at Mildred's. He's alive and he'll be ok, but this one," he pointed at Dirty, "he killed four men, in cold blood, and he'll hang for it . . . . Tomorrow."

"I'll be back, Dirty." Lizard said as he walked out the door.

"Ya mite not re-lize it, boy," Dirty said to the quivering lawman, "ya jist saved yer own life by telling' thet man whar 'is boy is. Iffen ya wuz real smart, ya'd git yer ass outten town fas' as ya kin. They's gonna be hell t' pay 'fore this is over."

The whore house was the one place in town that Donielle Bribois didn't mess with. He couldn't afford to get on the bad side of Mildred Barnes, the owner. If she got mad at him, she could cut-off services to his trappers. That particular service was one of the reasons they worked for him. He was the one who paid the madam, for the time they spent with her girls.

"They beat the hell outta him, sir." she told Lizard, "My girls rolled him on t' a blanket. Then it took all eight of us t' carry him in here. Ain't no way we'd git his big ol' butt up them stairs, so we fixed him a place in this back room. I sent Tim, the floor sweep in th' saloon, out to Doc Milton's and he came in and set his bones. Both arms, one laig, an' says he got ribs an' a coller bone broke, too. He finally woke up this mornin' an' ate like a damn cow. 'Scuse me ma'm, I ain't used t' havin' ladies 'round." she spoke gently to Red Bird. "I'm sorry 'bout th' bad language."

"You not worry, lady," Red Bird replied, "My husband trapper. He friends, trappers. They full of shit. Me know plenty bad talk."

Dick managed to smile at his mother's comment.

"Do you remember what happened to you, son?" Lizard asked.

"No, Paw, I just went into the saloon because Dirty told me to meet him there. A man who was picking on him earlier, walked up to me grinning. Next thing I knew, I was here, hurting like hell. That's all I know, Paw."

"That's alright, son, we're here, now, and your mother will take over your care." Lizard looked at Dick, then to Red Bird, "I've got to see how I can help Dirty out, and get all this mess straightened out." He took her small body in his big arms and held her for a minute. "He'll be ok, mother, he'll be ok."

Jeremy 'Lizard' Spencer pushed through the batwings of the saloon. He ordered whiskey, looked around, and saw only three other patrons. He straightened to his full height, walked to their table, laid three twenty dollar gold pieces on the table and softly said, "Would you gentlemen please be kind enough to leave this building for a few minutes? I need a little privacy."

The three grabbed a coin each, and scrambled out the door. Lizard walked back to the bar. "Were you here when my son got the hell beat out of him?" he asked the bartender.

"Naw, I didn't see nothing." was his answer.

Lizard leaned forward, over the bar. The bartender thought he was going to whisper something, and leaned toward Lizard.

Quick as a snake, Lizard grabbed the back of the bartender's head, slammed his face into the top of the bar, and told him, "Wrong answer! Now, were you here when my son was beaten?"

"Yeah! I was here." the man snatched a rag from behind the bar, wiped blood from his nose, and continued, "I don't know why that kid came in here, startin' trouble . . . .

Wham! "Owwww!" His face hit the bar again.

"I can do this all day, mister, can you?" Lizard asked.

"OKAY! OKAY! I saw what happen', I saw it all. Let go my haid an' I'll tell ya 'bout it."

Lizard turned the man's head loose, got hold of his shirt, and pulled him all the way over the top of the bar. "Whut're you doin'?" he whined.

"I'm sure you have a shotgun back there, right?"

The bartender nodded his head.

"Now, you still wonder why I want you on this side?"

The bartender shook his head.

"Good, now start talkin."

The town marshal walked up to saloon door, where Billy and Night Hawk were blocking the entrance. "Stand aside," he told them, "I'm the marshal here, and I need to see what's going on in there."

Night Hawk slid his black, obsidian knife from it's sheath, made one swipe at the front of the marshal's vest, and all four buttons fell to the dirt.

"What the . . . . ?"

His sentence was cut off by Billy's voice, "One of two things just happened, marshal. My brother might have taken a liking to you, because he could have laid your belly open, just as fast as he removed your buttons. Or . . . . You see, he's just fourteen, so he may have just missed. Either way, you won't disturb our father. He'll come see you when he's ready. Good day to you, sir,"

The marshal closed his gaping mouth, took the buttons from a smiling Night Hawk, who had picked them up, and walked away without a word.

"I always wanted to try that." Hawk told his brother, grinning. "I thought I could do it, with mom's glass blade. Next time I'll try it with my old steel. As thin as it is, it'll probably work."

'I'm glad I'm his brother.' Billy thought, *'I'd hate, like hell, to be his enemy."*

The bartender told Lizard, how Dirty and Dick had come into the bar earlier, that day. One of the frenchies had made some smart remarks about Dirty being a 'squaw man.' Fourteen year old Dick had told the older man to leave the 'poor old piece of buzzard bait' alone.

Dirty then told Dick to go to the store, to find out if Blue Bird's two rolls of material had arrived. Dick left the bar, Dirty turned to the trapper, who had been mouthing off, and told him to mind his own business. "Soon's we gits th' thangs my wife sent fer, we'z leavin'." Dirty swallowed his shot of whiskey, and walked from the bar.

Dick had returned a few minutes later. The same trapper walked to the bar, in front of him. Another trapper slipped in behind Dick, slugged him, in the head, with a club, and hit him again, as he fell to the floor. Two more joined them. They kicked, stomped, and clubbed the unconscious teenage boy, until Dirty screamed, from the door.

"Git 'way from 'at boy! Th' nex' man touches 'im is a daid man!"

The bartender continued his account of what happened next. "I ain't never seen nothing' like it. The frenchies turned 'round. One of 'em went fer his pistol, but before he could he could git it out, that ol' man's pig sticker hit him in the eye. Went right thru his haid, plumb to the hilt. 'Nother knife caught one of 'em in the throat. The ol' man had pistols in both hands by then. He pulled them triggers an' when the smoke cleared, all four of them bastards was daid."

He recounted the town marshal coming in, and asking what had happened. "All the ol' man told him was, 'jist cleanin' out a snake den.'" The marshal had asked Dirty to meet him at his office, to answer some questions. Dirty told him he was going to see to the boy's needs first. That was about the time Mildred and her girls came in, moved everyone aside and took over. "She sent Tim, my floor sweep, to git the doc, and her girls hauled the boy to the whore house. That's what I seen, mister. That's what happen' in here, but the marshal never asked me nuthin'."

Lizard went to the jail, to talk to Dirty. The exasperated marshal met him at the door. "Look what your son did to my vest, sir, he's ruined it."

"Buttons can be replaced, Marshal Vines, lives can't be. You told me earlier, that Mister Allen was going to hang tomorrow. May I see the court order to that effect?"

"Huh?" questioned the marshal. "Whut court order? We don't need a court order in Le Dereis. He killed four men, and he'll hang for it."

"Were you hired to enforce law in this town, marshal, or were you hired to hang people?

"The State of Wyoming, and the Constitution of The United States of America, states that John Allen is entitled to a fair trial. Is it your intention to hang him without one? If that is your intention, then I'll send one of my sons to get the judge in Jackson. My other son will watch you, marshal, every minute until the judge gets here. If you *are* going to let him have a fair trial, then *you* send for the judge. Either way, he'll have a trial, and I'll represent him.

"My name, sir, is Jeremy Spencer. I'm an attorney. I'll talk with my client, now, ... In private."

Marshal Vines took the cell keys with him and left.

"Hah!" Dirty said, "Ya shore got thet sumbich tongue tied. Hes b'lievin' all thet shit ya jist tol' him. He's prob'ly on his way t' th' post, t' see thet ad-je-tant feller. I found out it wuz his men I kilt. T' my thankin', thet law man works fer him, too."

"I wasn't feedin' him any shit, Dirty. I am an attorney. I just got tired of my practice back home, in Connecticut. That's why I came west. I fell in love with these mountains, as soon as I saw them, and decided to make my life in this wild, high country. I was down at Bent's more than twenty years ago, and there was a big man called Moose Parker there. He told me stories about beaver, ass-deep snow, Indians, bears and much more. I bought gear, then, and started making my way toward Wyoming. A couple years later, I met you . . . . and my Red Bird. That woman has taught me so much. I've been a lucky man, Dirty, with friends like you. Now, I'm gonna get you out of this mess. Tell me everything you know, and don't say another word to the marshal, or anyone else. I'll do all the talking, alright?"

"Wal I'll be damn, Lizard, ya big ox." Dirty stared at his friend. "I been wunnerin' 'ow come them boys talk so purty. Ya been teachin' 'em t' read an' 'rite, too?"

"Yes, Dirty, they can read, write, and do mathematics, that's the same as numbers. They can speak English, Arapaho, Cheyenne and use sign language. They also know the history of the United States, basic world history and can shoot as good, fight as hard, and use a knife as good or better than me, or most other grown men. And the best part, Dirty, is they're good boys. Now you tell me why my fourteen year old boy was in that saloon, and why he was beaten so badly."

Dirty told the story identically to that of the bartender, up to the point that Dirty went to the marshal's office. "Now ya know I'm a man what respects th' law, Lizard. Thet marshal, he tol' me he wanted t' see my weapons, then I could go t' see Dickey. I shoulda knowed better'n t' trust th' sumbich. Soon's I laid me knives 'n me guns on th' table, he got th' drop on me, 'n put me in this here cell. Tol' me I'ze gonna hang fer murderin' four o' th' town's leadin' citizens.

"They's beatin' the hell outten thet boy, Lizard, 'n I hollered fer 'em t' quit, 'n they drawed on me. Hell, they's jist stoopid frenchie trappers. They's cowerds! Ain't no way they's gonna win a fight 'gainst a real man. Thet's why they all worked t'gether on poor Dickey, Lizard, they's jist pure-dee cowerds. Th' basterds won' never pick a fight with 'nother kid."

As Lizard was leaving the jail, he met the marshal. The lawman had sent for the judge, in Jackson Hole. Depending on the judge's schedule, he could be there the next day, or it may be a few weeks. Lizard instructed the marshal that Dirty was to be fed good, and his cell was to be kept clean.

When the marshal began to object, Lizard reached out, rubbed the front of the buttonless vest and smiled. "Do you understand, Marshal?"

The marshal nodded.

"Hi Mom." Dick was happy to see his mother.

Red Bird was elated. "You no talk, Dick. You rest. You eat. You get well."

Mildred and her girls were like eight surrogate mothers. Dick's bandages, bed, and underwear were changed regularly. They helped him use a shallow pan, when he needed to relive himself. They explained to Red Bird that, because of their occupation, they were used to seeing naked men. Red Bird liked the women, and was thankful for their help. "There's a cot in the corner of the next room, m'am," Mildred told her, "Anytime you need to rest, my girls will look after him. I can't remember, ever, having a man in this house that was as nice as this boy. I wish I had a son just like him."

"Me got three boys." Red Bird said with pride. "All good sons. All big sons. All smart sons. You tell girls be careful, me boys han-some, too. Get under girls skirts." Red Bird and Mildred, both laughed, waking Dick.

"Ohh . . . . That hurts" he winced at a pain in his shoulder. "What's so funny? A man can't sleep around here with all that cackling going on. You two are worse than ol' Dirty, he snores all night, then makes you get up before daylight."

After the women visited with him for a while, he fell asleep again. The medicine, Doc Wilson had brought, was keeping the pain down to an acceptable level. Red Bird finally found the cot and rested, leaving her treasured son in capable hands.

Late the next day, Judge Charles Pendergrass drove his buggy into town. The marshal briefed him on the 'murders' and Dirty's trial was set for noon the following day. The saloon was the biggest room in town, and the bar served as the judge's bench. Dirty was brought to the 'courtroom' with hands bound, and a two foot length of rope tied to his ankles. The marshal seated nine men at the front tables. It was easy to tell all were French trappers, in the employee of Phillipe Brisbois.

As the judge called the court to order, a clean shaven, big man, dressed in a broadcloth suit and silk tie stood. Lizard spoke up. "Your Honor, I'd like to challenge the selection of these jury members. Many of them were close friends of the deceased men, and would be biased in their decision."

"I think I know you, sir," the judge was looking at Lizard with a question in his mind. "Are you Doctor Jeremy Spencer?"

"Yes, Your Honor, I am."

"And what are doing in this part of the country, Doctor Spencer?" asked the judge.

"I am defending my brother-in-law, and friend, John Allen, sir."

"The last time I saw you," added the judge, "was at Princeton University, teaching advance law students, who were interested in becoming justices, rather than practicing law."

"Yes, Your Honor, that's been many years ago. I've been living in Wyoming for more then twenty years, now. I've met many honorable men, here, and my client is one of the best. That is why I wish to challenge the selection of the jurists."

The judge dismissed all the jury members, and selected nine more from the crowd in the saloon. Just as the marshal began telling the judge and jury what, supposedly happened that fateful day, the batwings opened. A badly beaten Dick Spencer was being carried in, followed by a contingent of women. He was carried right to the front, close to the jury.

But the procession didn't stop there. Through the door came seventeen big, strong, bearded men. All were dressed in skins of various animals, were heavily armed, and had the look of seriousness. Their hats were a strange looking mix of military issue, heads or tails (or both) which once belonged to live skunks, bear, raccoon, or wolf . . . . old, mis-shapened felt cowboy hats, and one silk top hat, with half the brim missing.

These were the very essence of mountain men.

They stood, lining the walls on both sides of the door, so all present could see them, and vice versa. Through the door opening, you could see more of them on the outside, as though they were standing guard.

"What is this, Marshal?" Judge Pendergrass asked, "Do you know these men?"

The marshal was stuttering as Lizard spoke, "Your Honor, these men have known this injured young man, since the day he was born. They must have come here to watch, and see how real justice is accomplished." The last statement was to instill a feeling of competence in the judge's mind.

"You know all these men, then, Doctor Spencer." It was a statement, rather than a question.

There was some chuckling, coughing, and one outright 'HAW!', from the small army of big men, when the judge called Lizard 'Doctor Spencer'.

"Yes, Your Honor, in fact, the ugly one, with the eye patch, is my brother-in-law, James O'Donnel. Everyone else knows him as 'Skinner'.

My wife is the only person in these mountains who can skin a grizzly faster, and cleaner that he can. He'll probably disagree with that, but he disagrees with almost everything.

"The man to his left saved my life, four years ago, when I got hit by a nest, full of diamond back rattlesnakes. He doctored me for three weeks.

"The man with the skunk on his head, ... I think it's a dead one this time, . . . is Weasel Smith. He owned six lumber mills in Michigan, at one time. Now, he is married to the sister of a Nez Perce chief. He has also attained the rank of a sub-chief in their nation.

"When my son was beaten by four unscrupulous trappers, the man with the red feathers on his hat, rode day and night to inform me. He remounted and accompanied my family for a full day, then, I guess he started passing the word to more of my friends.

"I could tell you about each man standing over there. The stories would amaze you. But, Your Honor, everyone of them would lay down their life for a friend, or for what's right. None of them would ever, ever, do something like this to a fourteen year old boy. I will not recommend appointing any of them to the jury. They are friends with the defendant. And . . . . Most of them smell bad. It's best to leave them by the door and windows."

That brought another chuckle, and some grumbles, from the mountaineers.

Court was called to order, and the marshal continued to give his account, and opinion, of what happened on the day of the incident.

Lizard pointed out, that the marshal had not witnessed anything. He had arrived at the saloon as Dirty was collecting his knives. The only other witnesses were Dick, who was unconscious throughout the ordeal, and the bartender.

"The bartender ain't going to be tellin' anything, Judge." the marshal said, "A couple of boys found his body out back this mornin', with his throat cut." he looked at Lizard and continued, "That was the only one who witnessed the whole thing, Your Honor, so there's nobody else to say my account ain't as accurate as anyone's."

Dirty started to get up, but Lizard put his big hand on his shoulder, "Let me handle it, Dirty."

"Your Honor, if you'll indulge me for a few minutes, I'd like to find out something."

The judge granted Lizard the time. The mountain man/attorney turned to his two sons, who were standing behind him and Dirty.

"Boys, check the frenchies, find the one with fresh blood on his clothes, knife or any other evidence. We need to find the bartender's killer." He had spoken to them very quietly, so the crowd didn't realize what was going on, until Billy spoke up.

"Paw, this man has a smear of fresh, human blood on his pants."

The smaller French trapper jumped to his feet, and yelled, "Zis ees zee blood of zee deer I skeened zis morning. Zis boy ees a liar!"

Before the trapper knew what was happening, fifteen year old Billy had lifted him more than a foot off the floor, and had the tip of his own knife at the man's neck.

"Enough!," Judge Pendergrass called out, "Put that man down and holster that knife, young man."

Billy put away his blade, but carried the Frenchman to the front of the saloon. "Your Honor," he said, "deer blood turns dark brown within half an hour, in the dry air of this high country. It takes human blood three to four hours to turn dark. This man has human blood on his pants, where a knife has been wiped."

Lizard reached out and removed the trapper's knife from his belt, inspected it and handed it to the judge.

"As you can see, sir, there is still fresh human blood on his knife. Unless there is another body around here somewhere, this man killed the bartender, this morning."

"No, no!" the trapper squealed, "eet waz not me. Eet waz monsieur Brisbois! He tol' zee barteender to keep hee's mouth shut. Zee man said hee would tell zee truth. Monsieur Brisbois took mee blade, an' hee cut through zee neck of zee barteender. I deed not do eet, hee deed."

"Zat man ees not telling zee truth, Your Honoure. I am Fillipe Donielle Rene' Brisbois. I deed not keel eenyone. I am an out-stand-een ceetizen of thees town. I am zee owner of zee trading post, neer the north eend of town."

A booming voice broke in from the back of the room, "He don't own no tradin' pos', Judge. We saw it wuz on fire when we'z comin' in t' town. It prob'ly ain't nuthin' but ashes b' now."

As the commotion broke out, the mountain men blocked all the doors and windows. The judge beat the bar with his gavel, and called for order.

"This is the damndest case I've ever heard. We now have five dead men, two accusers, two suspects, a burned down trading post, a boy that was beaten, nearly to death, a little piss ant with a man's blood on his clothes and knife, another piss ant tooting his own horn about how respectable he is, a town marshal who jumps to conclusions, instead of getting facts, and the most brilliant law professor I've ever known, defending a stinky old man called 'Dirty', in a mountain town full of trappers and whores. Damn! Whose running this bar, anyway? I need a drink."

Tim, the saloon's floor sweep spoke up. "Yer Honor, the saloon's owned by a gent in Jackson. I guess I'm th' only workin' here, now. I'll be glad to get ya a drink, but kin I say somethin' first?"

"You better make it quick, son, I'm mighty dry." the judge replied.

"Well, the bartender weren't th' only one saw what happened that day. I saw it, too. I was in th' back corner, over there. I was skeered t' say anything. I gotta live here, an' these frenchies kin get bad if ya cross 'em. Those four hit th' boy in th' head, twice't, then they was stompin' him, beatin' him, an' kickin' him in th' ribs 'n tummy. That old man," he pointed at Dirty, "he hollered for them t' stop, an' they started drawin' their guns, before he did. He kilt 'em fair an' square, Judge. Th' other thang is, Mr. Brisbois an' this other one, was th' only ones here this mornin', an' took Mr. Buck, th' bartender, out back. Th' marshal came by, 'n went back there, too. I'll get ya that drink, now. What's yer pleasure?"

EPILOGUE

Fillipe Donielle Rene' Brisbois was hanged the next day.

Marcel Fontel, a trapper was hanged beside him. As Billy Spencer kicked the block from under him, he said, "You shouldn't have called me a liar."

Marshal Lemuel Vines filled a third noose.

The French Canadian trappers left Wyoming, traveling to north of the Canadian border, to find their game.

John 'Dirty' Allen returned home to his precious Blue Bird. He didn't like having killed the four men in that saloon, but wouldn't hesitate to do it again, but only if necessary. He lived in his valley, near Homer's peak, raising his horses, until his heart gave out at the age of seventy nine. His last request was that Blue Bird share his recipe for 'Black Bear Stew' with all who were interested.

The author has included it at the end of this epilogue.

Judge Charles Pendergrass resigned his position and bought the saloon, in which the trial had taken place.

Professor Jeremy 'Lizard' Spencer, and his family moved to Le Dereis, which had changed it's name to Riverbank, Wyoming. He built a big, new trading post, and was known far and wide as the fairest trader in the mountains. His son, Dick, recovered fully from his injuries. Four years later he became the town marshal of Riverbank. The previous marshal, Mack Dawkins, had just married Violet, one of the girls who had worked for Mildred.

Billy Spencer became a full fledged mountain man, and became as respected as his father. The speed, agility and strength he had displayed at the trial earned him nickname of 'Lightnin'.

Night Hawk Spencer moved back to the family's old home. He married the daughter of his mother's best friend, a beautiful Arapaho girl. They had six boys. The Spencer legacy would be passed down for a long time.

'Dirty's Black B'ar Stew

Wal, first'uv all, let me 'splain sump'in. It prob'ly taken me 'n Blue Bird ten, mebbe twelve yars t' work out this here res-pee.

We had sum purty bad batches tryin' t' figger out whut would make it jist rite.

Cupple o' times, she caught th' cabin on far, 'n once't the stew et plumb thru th' bottom o' th' pot. 'Course, her bein' a 'rapaho, she knows more 'bout cookin' dogs 'n porky-pines then she do b'ar.

Now, we fine'ly got it rite, so we d'cided t' let y'all know th' proper way t' cook 'Dirty's Black B'ar Stew'.

Ya got t' git all these thangs 'fore ya git started.

Ya got t' have 'nuff farwood fer a big far, thet'll las' two days. Ya got t' have one o' them big warsh pots, 'bout a twenny-five t' thirty gallun, cast 'arn pot. 'Course, ya needs t' clean it good, so's they's no soap left in it. Thet'd shore mess up th' stew.

Ya needs 'nuff water, from a sprang-fed creek, t' fill 'at pot three 'r four times. (Jist have yer woman keep all her carrin' jugs close, so's she won' have t' make mo' trips t' th' creek then she has'ta.)

Now, here's whut goes in it.

One mid-size black b'ar, 'bout two-fitty t' three hunnert ponnds. (If'n ya git a li'l un, it ain't got near 'nuff flaver, 'n a bigger'un won't fit in th' biggest pot ya kin git.)

'Bout twenny poun's o' taters. Them red'uns is best, but th' Iderho white'uns will work.

Ten 'er twelve o' th' biggest onions ya kin find at th' tradin' post. (If'n ya git 'em at Lizard's place, keep yer eye on 'im. He's a big dumb-ass, 'n he cain't count no good.)

Git a dubble handful o' garlic, the kind what grows wild near the high creeks, it ain't as bitter as whut th' trader's got.

Four big dried chilly peppers. I ain't never been able t' figger out jist why they calls 'em "chilly", 'cause they's hotter'n hell. Me 'n Blue Bird grows our own, but ya kin git 'em at the post, too.

'Bout nine er ten stalks o' roo-bob. Git th' young sprouts, th' ol' uns git too tuff.

Las' thang, git ' four t' five pounds o' them black beans. Th' Utes, o'er in Coloraddy grows th' bes' uns, but th' trader us'lly has sum gooduns, too.

Now, here's th' way I fixes it.
First, ya have yer woman skin the b'ar, trim mos' uv th' fat offen it, an' cut it up in fist-size chunks. This is th' hardest part, but a good woman kin git it done in a day, if'n she don' fart 'round. Don' let her thro' way th' fat. It'll come in handy fer other stuff.

She kin haul off all th' bones, 'n guts. This here stew takes so much time, they'd spoil 'fore she'd git time to do sump'in with 'em anyway.

She needs to put thet meat d'recly in th' pot, 'n git it b'ilin'. It takes a long time t' cook b'ar meat, rite. Git her t' put a bunch o' the fat in a fryin' pan, 'n let it melt 'til it starts t' burn. Then she kin set it t' th' side fer later.

While th' meat cooks fer 'bout four t' five hours, yer woman kin warsh the taters, 'n other stuff. Have her cut th' taters in 'bout five 'r six chunks 'n set 'em t' th' side.

Now, lots o' folks don' like roo-bob vurry much, so here's whut'cha do. I have Blue Bird t' cut thet stuff inter teeny weeny pieces, 'n pitch it in th' pot soon's th' meat gits cookin' good. Thet way, it cooks all t' pieces, 'n nobody even knows when they eats it. Th' flavor's kinda strong t' start, but by th' time ya add water a few times, it gits better.

Let th' meat 'n roo-bob cook all nite. Yer woman kin check th' far two er three times t' make shore it keeps cookin', n' add water.

First thang nex' mornin', she kin jist go 'head 'n pitch 'em black beans in th' pot, 'n scrape the burnt fat from th' other pan in t' it, too. Then she kin put th' taters 'n onions in. She'll need t' mash up th' garlic 'fore it goes in, 'n crush up th' peppers, 'til they's near 'bout a powder. Put it in, too.

This here part gits kinda tiresum. It's a lotta work fer one woman, so it's best t' have one o' her sisters, er mebbe a friend, t' hep out. Ya gotta keep thet far burnin' purty hot, *AN'*, ya hafta stir purt-near all th' time, 'til it's all mushed up 'n ya kin lite a suffer match, by jist throwin' it in th' pot.

Jist b'fore it gits dark, set th' pot offen th' far. Jist 'member t' be keerful, thet stuff's been cookin fer two days, 'n it's so thick, it'll take a site o' waitin' 'fore it cools down.

Thet's it! Thet's how I cooks black bear stew. Not much left to do. Jist let it cool o'ernite. Blue Bird us'ully sleeps outside, clost t' th' pot. That way, no varmits will git in it.

Now fer th' mos' importan' part. Next mornin', y'all kin carry the pot full o' stew t' the creek bank. Jist dump it all in th' creek, 'n ya ain't gonna b'leve how damn many fish'll jump plumb out on t' th' bank, tryin' t' git away from thet crap.

Yer woman's gonna be able t' fix fish fer ya, all kinda ways, fer th' nex' week.

If Ya Cain't Run With The Big Dogs . . .

The big, skinny dog stood, yawned, and wagged his tail. He'd been wagging it for the last two days, but hadn't been able to stand.

Clifford Evans had found the sick Great Dane a week ago, when he heard the other one barking. The healthy dog didn't want Cliff to come near her friend, even though she had barked for a full day, trying to attract help.

It had taken Cliff several minutes to calm the protector, to the point he could examine the fallen one. A dark wound on the dog's front leg, with two small punctures, was a definite indication that it had been in a confrontation, . . . with a rattlesnake.

Cliff had been in southeastern Colorado for fourteen years, and was fully aware that, many animals had a higher tolerance to the venom, than most humans did.

As Cliff laid the big, unconscious dog across the back of his horse, the other one pranced up to him carrying the remains of a very large, western diamondback. The big snake had done damage, but had also paid the price. Cliff gave a command to 'get back'. The dog obeyed, immediately, without hesitation.

He managed to get the limp dog secured, convinced the other one to leave her prize, and headed back towards his ranch house.

Cliff's wife, Dottie, saw him riding in with a monstrous dog beside his horse, and something nearly as big behind his saddle. "What in the world's going on, Cliff? Is that a dog? I've never seen a dog that big. Is that another one?" she pointed at the limp carcass behind him.

"Yep, Dot, they're both dogs. I think they're called Great Danes. I've never seen one either, but I've heard about 'em. This one took a hit from a rattler, but he's still alive." *He pointed at the female and continued,* *"She must've killed the thing. It was a big'un, too, Dot, ... had eleven rattles on it's tail. Think you can doctor this one back to life?"*

Dottie made a bed in the barn, from old saddle blankets, and forced water, and fresh milk, down the dehydrated dog's throat, using the syringe on a hot water bag. She told Cliff that the female dog seemed to answer to the name 'Girl'. Naturally, she started calling the sick one 'Boy'.

Now, Boy was finally able to get up, onto his huge feet. Dottie had taken notice how tough and leathery their paw pads were. They hadn't had a soft life, and they were friendly enough, but, the nagging questions were, where did they come from, and who did they belong to.

Girl ate good, but was always watching for Boy to get up and eat, too. He made an attempt to walk to the feed bucket, and fell.

Dottie helped him to his feet, but he fell again. Finally, on the third try, he took six steps, laid down next to the bucket, and proceeded to help himself to Girl's leftovers. After a good meal of cornmeal mush, with beef scraps in it, Boy was back on his feet, stretching muscles he hadn't used in several days.

The bucket of water was next, then he made his way back to his bed. A little more than an hour later, he was romping in the yard, with Girl.

"You've done a good job, sweetheart," Cliff told Dottie, as she and their Mexican house keeper, Conchita, were watching the action from the porch. "Now, what are we goin' to do with these two? I'm not sure we can afford to feed 'em. It'd be different if they'd eat grass and hay."

"Girl gets along fine with 'Chita and the ranch hands." Dottie said. "She plays with the other dogs, and doesn't chase the cats, nor the chickens. Someone trained her well, and so far, Boy acts the same way."

Girl stopped short as she was trotting across in front of them. She looked toward the gate and a low growl began in her throat. Boy ran to her side, looked the same direction, and barked once. Within a minute, a lone rider came over the hill, heading for the ranch.

"C'mere, Girl, C'mere, Boy." Cliff called to them. They spun around, ran directly to his side, sat, and watched the rider approach.

Cliff's sister, Nancy, rode through the gate and halted at the hitch rail.

Another growl came from Girl. Cliff patted her head, and told her "It's alright, Girl, it's just Nancy. She kinda cantankerous, sometimes, but she's welcome here. Be good, now."

Boy raised, wagged his tail, and made his way, slowly, to the newcomer. Nancy was only about two feet taller than the dog, and reached to pet him. Boy stopped and, hesitantly, stuck his nose toward her outstretched hand.

"Well hello there big boy, who are you?" Nancy asked the curious dog. "You're a pretty thing, but how come you're so skinny? Won't Cliff and Dot feed you?"

Nancy's hand rubbed against the big dog's nose, then moved up to it's ears. She scratched the top of his head, and Boy felt like he'd tamed another human.

Another indication the dogs had been trained well, was that they never licked anyone, nor raised their front feet up onto someone's body. To do so could be dangerous to a person as small as Nancy.

Girl watched as Boy made a connection with the newcomer. Soon, it was too much for her to take. She decided that she wanted her head scratched, also. It took a total of ten minutes before Nancy could move on to greet Cliff and Dottie.

Hugging her sister-in-law, she asked, "Well, it looks like you two have a couple of new additions to the family. I was hoping for nieces and nephews, but not ones this big. Where'd you get them?"

Cliff told the story as the dogs took off to chase a poor jackrabbit, which had run out from behind the house. Girl was on the rabbit in seconds, with Boy on her heels.

"Wow," Nancy interrupted, "Look at them run!"

"Boy still can't move very fast. Think of what he can do, once he is healthy, again." Cliff said, "I'm going into La Junta tomorrow to ask around about them. They belong to somebody, and I'm sure that same somebody is wondering where they are."

"If you can't find the owner, will you keep them?" Nancy asked.

"I really like them," Dottie answered, "I kind of hope we don't find the owners. I would love to keep them."

"Well, I guess they can feed themselves," Cliff said, pointing, "They just caught their own dinner, that jack didn't have a chance. At least there's plenty of rabbits, ground squirrels, and prairie dogs around. I'd like it fine if they'd clean out the damn prairie dogs."

"Well, I like them, too, Dot." Nancy said, "but it would be a shame if there's somebody, out there, that loves them and misses them. But . . . . There's a more important reason I rode out here, today." She pulled her riding gloves off and held her left hand out, for inspection. "You're looking at the, soon to be, Mrs. Doctor Jeffery Melton."

"Nancy! How wonderful!" Dottie exclaimed, as she examined the engagement ring, "When did all this happen? . . . AND . . . When is the big day?"

Cliff, not wanting to get involved in 'women's talk', walked toward the barn, telling the ladies he'd be back in a little while.

Nancy told Dottie all about the developments in her love life. Doctor Melton had been in La Junta three years, now, and had talked Nancy into a date, three weeks ago. They had seen each other every day since then, except once, when he had to make an overnight trip to the Jensen's place, for Betty Jensen's labor and the delivery of a big healthy baby boy. Just yesterday he asked Nancy to marry him. The wedding would take place in two weeks, as soon as his mother could make the trip from St. Louis.

Dottie had never seen Nancy so happy, since the death of her, and Cliff's, parents, who were killed four years ago, when lightning hit their buggy. They were on their way to town, to visit Nancy, who had just landed a job working in the land office. Several large bolts of lightning struck the area that day, but not a drop of rain had fallen. The freak storm left their parents' matched set of young Morgan horses dead, also. Travelers found the grisly scene, the following morning. For a long time, Nancy felt like the tragedy was her fault, because they were coming to see her.

She was happy, now, and agreed to spend the night at her big brother's house. She would ride back with him, tomorrow, as he went to La Junta.

Cliff called to the women, told them he was riding out to check a pasture fence, and mounted his, green broke, bay colt. "Y'all don't wait for me. Soon as 'Chita says your supper's ready, go ahead and eat. I'll get mine when I get back, it shouldn't be long."

Girl and Boy decided to go, too, and fell in behind him. He pulled up, turned in his saddle, and spoke, "Stop!" . . . the dogs stopped. "Set!" . . . the dogs sat. "Stay!" he gigged the young horse in the ribs and trotted through the gate.

Looking over his shoulder, he smiled as he saw the two Great Danes watching him, but still sitting where he told them. Ordinarily, Cliff wouldn't mind the dogs' being with him, but a young, green broke, colt needs full time attention. He didn't want to take a chance on the dogs spooking his mount. A few more outings, on this one, and he would be much more comfortable. He also figured that Boy need more time recuperating, anyway.

After forty-five minutes, Cliff found a broken fence wire and dismounted. As he put his weight on his right foot, it twisted on a rock, causing him to shout an expletive. The horse shied, causing him to fall. Luckily, his left boot came out of the stirrup, but the horse left, at a dead run. A few minutes later, Cliff found the remnant of an old fence post and, using it as a cane, started hobbling toward home.

It was nearing sunset when the colt trotted back into the yard. Girl started barking, and didn't stop until Dottie came out the front door. Seeing the riderless horse, she knew Cliff had been thrown. "Whipper!" she shouted at the foreman, who was in the corral, "Something's happened to Cliff! Saddle my horse and bring some other men, we've got to go find him!"

Cliff heard Boy's barking, long before anyone could see his form, silhouetted in the light of the rising moon. Dottie had brought a pair of his dirty overalls, held them to the dogs' noses, then fell in behind the pair, as they left the ranch at a run. Evidently, Boy had sensed Cliff was close and started barking, as they closed the distance at an unbelievable pace. Once the dogs spotted him, Girl passed Boy, and flew the last fifty yards, to Cliff's side.

They both gave whimpers, and yips, of joy as they bounded around him. By the time Dottie and the other riders reached the excited trio, the dogs had settled down, and Cliff was petting them. Using Girl for support, he started moving, again, toward the oncoming rescue party.

"Hey! Over here!" he yelled and waved the large stick. Cliff was amazed at the stamina Boy was showing, considering the dog was barely able to stand earlier in the day.

"Whut's goin' on, Boss?" Whipper asked, "Did ya decide ya'd send th' hoss home 'n git yer exercise by walkin' back?"

Before Cliff could respond, Dottie interrupted, "Well, that's one horse we'll be getting rid of. If he can throw *you*, we don't need to be keeping him."

"Now, Dot," Cliff saw the worried look on his wife's face. "He didn't throw me. In fact, he rode out really well. I was already dismounting when

I twisted my ankle and I yelled, right next to his ears. Don't blame him, it was my fault. I think he's gonna be a good mount. We'll keep him and call him Smarty, 'cause he was smart enough to go get you."

He knelt between the Great Danes, and continued, "And, speaking of smart, you two are something else." Cliff rubbed behind their ears, down their necks, and across their backs, "I hope like hell, nobody does show up to claim you."

Before leaving for La Junta, the next day, Cliff told Whipper to take another man, go back to the west fence line, and repair the broken top wire. "Ya wan'us ta take a hammer 'n bust thet li'l ol' rock thet hurt yer ankle, too?" Whipper was always teasing his boss, but Cliff had total confidence in his well seasoned foreman.

"Nope," Cliff answered, "I wouldn't want you to strain yourself. It's been forty years since you did any real work. Swinging a hammer might do you in for good, then I'd have to train another foreman."

"Wal, Mister Evans, . . . sir, . . . I wasn't goin' t' swing it, anyway. I'ze gonna have Deuce do th' work, with me supa-vizin. Now, do ya need me ta hep ya git in thet buggy?"

Against his better judgment, Cliff accepted the help, climbed into the buggy, and extended Nancy a hand. Deuce had already tied her horse behind the rig, and placed her saddle behind the seat.

"I'll be back before supper, Sugar," he told Dottie, "and I'll be hungry."

Dottie called to the dogs and told them to 'stay', as Cliff and Nancy drove away. Girl was especially anxious to be with Cliff, but after Dottie patted their heads, and talked to them for a few minutes, they seemed content to stay at the ranch. They watched as Whipper and Deuce rode out toward the west fence, then went for a romp behind the house, probably looking for another rabbit.

"Miz Dottie! Miz Dottie!" Whipper's yelling brought Dottie out of the house, as he rode in. "Miz Dottie, how soon's th' boss gonna be back? We got a big problem, Miz Dottie. It looks like we'ze got rus'lers. Th' fence wuz cut, all four wires. Ya kin see whar th' rascals drove 'em cows right thru 'n headed north."

The men had been gone for about two hours when Whipper had returned. It was only a thirty minute ride to town, so Dottie told the other hand, Dusty, to ride to the nearest neighbors, at the Circle-M. She told him to get Buddy Morris, and all his available hands, and go directly to the cut in west fence. Whipper was to change mounts, and return there, too. Dottie would ride to town, find Cliff and the sheriff, and meet all of them at the same place.

As Whipper rode out, Dottie turned to the Great Danes, "Go with Whipper! Go! Go with Whipper!" They looked at her with uncertainty, but when Whipper called "c'mon", the dogs took off, and were matching the pace, set by the horse.

"Yep, the wire's been cut aw-right." the sheriff told Cliff, "They must've seen you ridin' up yesterday, and lit out. Prob'ly hid in them trees over yonder. After the rest of your folks found you and headed home, they must've figured y'all wouldn't be back out this way for a few days. They came back, finished cuttin' the fence, and headed your stock toward Wyoming. I guess we'll head out after 'em, but first, we need t' get somethin' straight. *I'm* the one in charge. I'll listen to anything y'all have to say, but *I'll* make the decisions. I'm not gonna have a lynch mob on my hands. If we catch these bastards, 'scuse me Miz Dottie, *I'll* decide what's gonna happen to 'em."

Dusty and one of the Morris hands were good trackers. They rode out ten minutes before the rest of the group. Cliff and Whipper figured the cattle taken, numbered close to one hundred twenty head. That large a herd left a pretty clear trail. Two more Morris hands arrived with another buggy. They had loaded it with supplies, a portion of which was transferred to Cliff's buggy. Ordinarily, no buggies were used on an undertaking like this, but, considering how quickly the crime was discovered, and how fast this posse was assembled, it wasn't expected to be a long pursuit.

Girl and Boy rode in the buggy with Cliff and Dottie, but jumped down and trotted beside them part of the time. "Did you have a chance to find out anything about their owner?" she asked Cliff.

"I didn't have much time, but the sheriff sent a couple of wires, and I left notes at some of the businesses. We'll see what turns up."

About four, in the afternoon, Girl stopped suddenly, and barked once. Cliff stopped the rig, watched the horizon and soon saw Dusty, riding toward them. The troupe came to a halt and waited.

Dusty rode on in and reported that they had located the rustlers, and the livestock, at a makeshift corral less than two miles ahead. "They mus' be purty pleased with theyselves, they ain't even got a lookout. Either that or they's just dum-asses. Oh, sorry Miz Dottie. They got a fire goin' an' they's awreddy usin' a runnin' iron on th' brands, changin' the 'E-bar' t' a 'B-cross'. They ain't doin' a very good job, neither. Must be they first job."

The sheriff paired up the men, and gave them specific directions on how he wanted the rustlers surrounded. They moved out, quietly, and made their way toward the outlaws' camp. Cliff and Dottie stayed with the buggies, but Whipper took Girl with him. Being over six feet tall, Whipper didn't bend an inch as he petted the long legged canine, "C'mon with me, Girl, jist be good 'n ya stay right with me." he patted his leg, "We's gonna go git them bad actors, 'n see to it they don' pull this shit, agin."

"Stay here, Boy" Dottie spoke in a low tone, "We'll just wait. Whipper and Girl will be ok." Although Boy was standing beside the buggy, his head was higher than Dottie's seat. She had her left arm lying on his back.

Fifteen minutes later, Boy's head snapped around, his ears perked up and he started a low growl. Turning in his seat, Cliff saw a rider approaching, with his rifle trained on him and Dottie. "Easy, Boy," Cliff spoke softly, "easy." Dottie clenched a handful of skin on Boy's neck, and repeated the command, herself.

Dottie told Cliff to be ready to go for his gun, because the man was on the opposite side of the rig from Boy, and may not have seen the dog. Cliff thought *'how could anyone not see him, as big as he is?'*

When the rider came within twenty feet, Dottie released her grip and said, "Get him, Boy!" The gunman yelled "What the . . . !?" as he saw the monstrous dog racing toward him. The distraction gave Cliff time to swing his Winchester up, and told the man to drop his guns. Just as he looked back at Cliff and Dottie, Boy leapt, knocked the rider from his saddle, and stood over him, eye to eye, growling.

"If you even touch one of your guns, mister, you are a very, very dead man." Cliff told him, calmly. "I'll blow your brains out, unless ol' Big Boy beats me to it by tearing out your throat."

"No . . . . Please!" the wide eyed young man cried out, "Please . . . git this thang off me. I ain't touchin' no guns . . . . Jist git him off!"

Dottie climbed down, went to the downed outlaw, took his weapons and stepped away. "C'mon, Boy, come over here." Boy backed off moved to Dottie's side. "You don't move an inch, mister, or I'll sic him right back on you. You got him covered, Cliff?"

"Yeah, I got him, Dot. Get the rope, here, and tie him. Watch him, Boy."

Just as Dottie finished tying the stranger, they heard shouting and two shots rang out. Boy jumped and looked toward the direction on the rustlers' camp. "Go, Boy, go!" Cliff told him. Boy looked at him, Cliff said "go" again, and the dog took off at a hard run.

As Boy ran into camp, he went straight to Whipper. "Where ya been, ya lazy ol' flea bag? Me 'n Girl, here, done rounded up th' whole gang o' rus'lers. Th' sheriff 'n th' others are gittin' 'em on they hosses, now." When Whipper realized that he had just started a conversation with a dog, he cleared his throat, looked around to see if anyone else had heard him, and whispered, "C'mon, let's git back t' th' boss, 'n tell him he kin c'mon in, now."

The tall, lanky cowboy, and the two tall, lanky dogs were a welcome sight to the young couple. "How'd it go, Whipper? Did you have to take charge and capture the rustlers all by your self?" Cliff asked.

"Nope, this here girl pup bit one of 'em in th' ass 'n made him fall down. I got th' rest'uv 'em though. Ya jist cain't d'pend on other folks, no matter how nice 'n willin' they is. Thet ol' sheriff'll prob'ly give me a medal er sumthin. Ennyways, it's safe fer y'all t' come in, now, th' sheriff's decidin' whut he's gonna do with 'em."

Dottie and Cliff chuckled, told Whipper what had happened to them, and touched the whip to the horse pulling the buggy. Whipper led the other rig, as well as the captured rustler, who was tied to his horse.

The small posse assembled at the edge of the camp. The three men, captured in the act of changing brands on stolen cattle, were pronounced guilty without question. Seven men, including the county sheriff, had witnessed that crime.

After the sheriff listened to Cliff's account, the fourth outlaw was lined up under the same large oak limb. Four ropes were thrown over it, nooses were tied around four necks, and four horses were slapped from under the men.

Graves were dug and the rustlers had been put out of everybody's mind. The facts were quite simple. The crime had been committed, and justice had been administered, in accordance with the code of the west. After the burial, not another word was mentioned about the four young men, whose lives ended as the results of bad choices.

Supper, that night, was an interesting experience for Dottie. Although she'd been raised around men, all her life, she'd never spent several hours around a campfire with a bunch of well seasoned wranglers, who were trying to outdo each other with their tales and insults. Not wanting to spoil their fun, she tried to stay as far from the fire (and their comments), as the cool Colorado night would permit.

Occasionally, the conversation would get around to the subject of women. "I jist cain't unnerstan' wimmin." one whiskered old timer commented, "They wants ya ta warsh yer hands 'n face 'fore ya eat. Ya cain't come in ter th' house, iffen ya got cow shit on yer boots. They 'spect ya ta open th' door fer 'em, 'n hep 'em up in ter a buggy, even ef they don' need no hep. Iffen ya don' do thangs the way they wants, they gits mad, or starts cryin'."

"Quit yer whining', Pete." Whipper told him, "Yer awmost sixty yars ol' 'n ya ain't got wimmin figgered out yet! It's easy! They's jist like th' weather, ya cain't do nuthin 'bout it, so ya jist do whut it takes t' put up with it. Th' smartest thang ya kin do, 'course I know ya, Pete, 'n ya ain't too smart, is jist tell her 'yes ma'm'. Thet way ya kin git in the last word. Then ya go 'head 'n do whut she wants."

"Aww, shet yer yap, Whipper, ya don' know nuttin 'bout wimmin, 'cept how t' git in they britches. Oh!, sorry miz Dottie, I fergot ya wuz over there." That was just one of several apologies Dottie received that night. She really didn't mind the language, much, and the chuckles she got were more than enough to make up for it.

She and Cliff spread their bedroll under their buggy. They lay together and laughed at the barbs being exchanged by the others. Frequently, the effects of the evening's meal, beans and bacon, were heard, which prompted more comments and insults. Eventually, everyone settled down, but the beans continued to work themselves out all night long.

After breakfast the next morning, which was mainly leftovers from the night before, plus some hot sourdough biscuits, Buddy Morris and the Circle M hands, fell in quickly to help the E-Bar men move the cattle back to their home range. Whipper led the drive to the same place where the wire had been cut, and the herd was slowly pushed through. That being accomplished, the Morris men headed home, and Whipper's men fixed the fence.

As Cliff and Dottie drove through the main gate, they were greeted to a sight they hadn't anticipated. It appeared as though an eight-legged, two-headed Great Dane was looking at them.

"Well, it looks like Girl will be having pups in a couple of months." Cliff observed. "Even if we find their owners, maybe we can get one of their offspring. It's amazing, to me, the intelligence of those two. My ankle's feeling better, now, so I'll make another ride into town in a couple days. Maybe there's been some response to one of the wires."

"I hope not, Cliff, I really love those dogs." She patted her stomach and continued, "the puppies will be weaned just about the same time your son gets here."

Cliff stopped the rig, set the brake and grabbed his wife in a hug. "What?? When?? How long have you known?" Dottie laughed, answered his questions and started out of the buggy. "Wait, I'll help you!" Cliff insisted.

"I'm fine, Cliff, women get pregnant every day. I won't break. Besides, I heard Pete and Whipper's remarks, last night about women. If you go helping me do everything, they'll be making those comments about you. 'Chita is all the help I'll need, you just go on and do your 'man' chores. I'll be fine."

Cliff drove the rig to the barn, told Dusty the good news, and continued to the bunkhouse. He wanted to share the news, as soon as the rest of his crew arrived. However, knowing them as well as he did, *they'd* probably be more excited about the prospect of pups.

Cliff checked with the sheriff, in La Junta. No wires had been returned about the lost Great Danes, but one had come in asking about a Redbone coon hound, and another inquiring about a crate of chickens, which were dropped from a freight wagon near Denver. Those probably wound up as coyote food.

"Let's head for home, Girl," he said as he bent to pet his dog, who had accompanied Cliff to town that day, "We'll stop at the bank first, then pay Mr. Cotton at the hardware store. We'll still get home in time for dinner. Dottie said she'd fry some chicken, and I'd love to get back while it's still hot." He bent slightly, scratched Girl behind the ears, with both hands, and continued, "But, if we wait much longer, I'll probably wind up eating the leftovers, cold, for supper. C'mon."

Girl laid beside a water trough, outside the bank. The drip from the seams kept the dirt, close to the trough, wet and cool.

Cliff went inside, withdrew fifty dollars, thanked the teller and started out the door. Just as he stepped outside, two men, with guns in their hands and bandanas covering their faces, forced him back through the door. Cliff saw, immediately, what was going on and called out, "Girl, Help!"

The outlaw wheeled, grabbed Cliff by the front of his shirt, and barely managed to say "Shut up!" when a large set of teeth clamped onto his shoulder. The ensuing scream, as he was being thrown to the floor by the huge dog, caused total disruption in the bank.

His partner, who had gone directly to the teller's window, turned quickly to see what was happening. The quick thinking teller pulled the sawed off ten-gauge from the lower shelf and told the man to drop his gun. When the robber swung his pistol back, toward the teller's window, the big blast took off the man's hand and blew a hole in his chest.

The first outlaw, who Girl had pinned to the floor, tried to raise his pistol, but Cliff stomped the man's hand, causing the gun to fall free. When Cliff screamed out in pain, Girl clamped her teeth onto the man's neck. "Back, Girl" Cliff yelled. Girl released the man, but not before blood was leaking from the front of his neck.

Cliff called Girl to his side, told her to sit, and caught a handful of her neck skin. She was anxious and confused for the next few minutes, with customers running out, and the sheriff, the town marshal, and two deputies, running in.

"What the hell's going on, Robert?" the sheriff asked the teller.

As the man recounted the happenings of the last five minutes, the two deputies handcuffed the man on the floor.

"Better get him a doctor, boys, one that can treat dog bites." Cliff advised.

"Robert tells me you called your dog in, but he said you screamed pretty loud, too." said the sheriff.

"Yeah, I stomped that son-of-a-bitch's hand with my sore ankle. It hurts worse, now, than it did when I twisted it, four or five days ago. I Guess I was pretty loud. I'll get Girl to help me to the doc's place, and have him look at it. He'll be my brother-in-law, sometime next week. Maybe he won't be tied up too long, with that other ol' boy." Cliff chuckled and said, "Girl worked his ass over like he was a rag doll. I'm glad she likes me."

"I'll tell you this for sure, Cliff," the sheriff said, "If you ever turn bad, and I have come looking for you, I'll hope like hell that monster's in the next state. I damn sure don't want to be on her bad side." the man squatted and spoke to Girl, "You are my friend, aren't you, Girl?"

Girl gave Cliff a quick glance, then took two steps toward the sheriff. She was quick to nuzzle his outstretched hand, and inclined her head, in a manner that suggested an ear scratch.

"You're a good girl." the ear scratch was working well. "If Cliff ever decides to get rid of you, you can stay with me. My wife and son would love you to pieces."

Cliff told him that, if nobody claimed the dogs, there was a litter of pups on the way, and he was first in line, if he wanted one. He did.

EPILOGUE

Eleven long-legged puppies were born two months later. There was a waiting list of people, wanting an offspring of the big, tan dog, who spoiled the bank robbery. Those who were not in line for the first litter, anxiously waited for the next batch.

The sheriff never told Cliff nor Dottie about the telegram, he received, from a gambler in San Francisco, claiming he lost a pair of Great Danes at a train stop in Colorado.

Nancy Evans and Doctor Jeffery Melton were married in La Junta, Colorado, on June 16, 1890. Between the Meltons and the Evans, eight children were raised in the rich farm and ranch lands of southeastern Colorado.

The beautiful Great Dane, everyone just called her 'Girl', gave birth to ninety-seven puppies, over an eleven year period. Her mate, Boy, died in April, 1902, three days after Girl had. Their descendants can still be found, within sight of the Rocky Mountain foothills.

'Gator Shoes'

"Davey boy, 'd I ever tell you 'bout the time your Unc' Zeke and me got in the 'gator bizness?" Gramps had his eyes closed and was re-living the past, again. He was nearly 90 years old. He had told me the stories about all the shenanigans he, and his brother Ezekiel, had been involved in, as they 'tamed' the American wilderness. In fact, over the last year or so, I'd heard most of them several times. His thoughts were never in the present, anymore, but mostly were in the 1850's and '60's.

The stories, actually, were interesting, but there was no doubt they were "enhanced" a little, with each telling.

"I don't think you told me that one, Gramps." I didn't have a problem listening to the tales he spun. If, in fact, those two had done everything he told about, Uncle Zeke would have had to be 140, when he died. That would make Gramps about 148, now.

Both of them were just teenagers when they left Kentucky. They stayed together all their life, until Zeke died three years ago. Gramps took it pretty hard at first, but soon decided that the whole family needed to know about their adventures.

Now he spends most of his time in his rocking chair, telling stories on the wide front porch of the two story house, the two of them built, in northern California, near the mountains.

Gramps and grandma lived in the downstairs rooms, and Uncle Zeke, with his wife Little Dove, a Ute Indian, lived upstairs.

Now, my mother, Celeste, Gramps' first daughter, and my dad, Will Baxter, lived upstairs. I lived downstairs, with Gramps.

"Well, han' me a dip from thet can o'r there, 'n I'll let you in on the dangdest tale you ever heered." As I handed him the snuff can, I remembered that Grandma had told me about Zeke getting in trouble at school, when he was about 13. He got caught peeking through a knot hole in the outhouse wall, while some little girl named Jenny was inside. The teacher wore his backside out with a paddle, and promised to tell his paw about it, too.

"Jake", he had said to Gramps, "I ain' letting' paw whoop my ass ag'in. Last time he whooped me, he bust'd me so hard, I had reach o'er my shoulder to wipe my butt".

Zeke then proceeded to talk Gramps, Jacob Waldo Jefferson, into running away from their Kentucky home. Jake knew that there was no way to talk Zeke out of it, but he felt like Zeke was too young to go alone. Their long journey had begun.

"Yep, a'ter we worked a coupl' yeers on the docks in St. Louie, we got a purty good stake up an' had it hid in the mat'ress at th' roomin' house.", he started. "Now ol' Zeke, he'd been watchin' lots o' people gittin' on & off the riv'rboats. They wuz a bunch o' 'em wearin' shiny shoes, an' Zeke ask'd 'em 'bout thet. They said they's made outta 'gator skin, but they cos' as much as three or four dollars a pair."

"Anyways, we got t' talkin' an' we decides t' head down th'ol' Mississip' t' Lewsiannie, whar th' 'gators live. We figgered if'n them shoes cos' thet much, a whole hide must brang a purty penny, so, we'd jist go down riv'r, ketch us a bunch o' them gators, skin 'em out and git rich."

Gramps was a man who never backed away from work. He could, and did, the work of any two men, no matter what job he took on. Uncle Zeke didn't mind working hard, but his strong suit was the gift of gab, and making deals. Zeke was smarter, bigger and stronger than most fifteen year old boys. Seeing the two of them side-by-side, an observer wouldn't believe there was nearly five years difference in their ages. As a benefit of Zeke's good looks and sweet-talking, it seemed like there were always ladies around, for both of them.

"Well, Davey boy, once't we hit New Orleens, we seen thangs we n'er even thought of."

Gramps always called me 'Davey boy'. A few times I mentioned that he could just call me 'Davey', or even 'Dave', like everyone else does, but he never changed.

"They wuz buildin's thar they said wuz two hunnert yeers old. Big ol' churches thet'd hol' a hunnert people 'er more. Zeke an' me, we never seen enythang like it, even in St. Louie." Gramps chuckled and said, "Ya know, they's even cemetarys down thar thet is all on top o' the ground. Says they's not able to burry 'em in the ground, 'cause they hits water, soon's they start diggin'. Zeke liked to tell folks, 'bout how they wuzn't 'llowed to let anyone livin' within a mile o' one of them places, to be burried there . . . . *THEY HAD T'BE DAID FIRST!*"

Gramps cackled for a minute, then just sat let his mind wander. In a few minutes, he started in again. "We found out we's gonna have t' go east & south o' New Orleens, t' git t' the swamps where mos' the gators were. We headed out and got plum' eat up by skeeters. Y' ain' never seen so many o' 'em. They's so thick, we had t' walk our hosses backerds, so's their tails'd brush a path thru 'em. Ain' never seen 'em so big, neither. When we could, we'd kill us one, 'n it wuz big 'nuff t' feed both o' us fer supper. Now, Davey boy, you mite thank I'ze joshin' ya, but I swear I saw one, with my own eyes, 'nock Zeke plum off'n his horse. An' Zeke rasseled thet thang 'round on the ground 'til he killed it with his skinnin' knife. I bilt a fire t' smoke the rest o' 'em away, and we cooked the daid one. Tast'd lots like chik'n.", he chuckled.

He went on to tell about the 'funny talkin' people in the swamps. They were called 'cajuns', and pushed a small boat, Gramps said they called it a 'pee-row', through the shallow water with stout poles. There were different ways that the 'cajuns' killed alligators, but the method Zeke and Gramps were going to use, was, to 'rope' the jaws of the animal, then straddle it and put a bowie knife through the vulnerable spot, in the top of it's head. It was quick, sure, and didn't damage the valuable skin.

"I 'member the first 'un we got. I has me a thin stout rope, 'n when we slid the pee-row 'long side thet ol' gator, I din't have no problem ketchin' the jaws. Ya see, they ain' got no power openin' they mouth. It's easy t' hold it closed, 'cause all they strenth is in chompin' down. Anyway, Zeke figgered that, quick as I'd roped 'is mouth, he'd jump on it and git his knife in it's head. Well, boy, thet ol' gator, he had diff'rent idees. He started whuppin' 'is tail an' head in diff'rent d'rections. Zeke wuz hit by the end o' the tail, first, 'n wound up in th' knee-deep water with th' wrong end down. Hah! When he got back up, thet 'gator wuz a'pullin' me an' th' pee-row t'other way.

"Jist as Zeke caught up with us, soaked t' th' bones and cover'd with mud, two o' them cajuns showed up 'n a 'nuther pee-row. Them ol' boys wuz laffin' at us, an' I guess it wuz a funny site, but it didn' set well with Zeke. He wuz proud o' his idee 'bout huntin' 'gators, an' he's wantin' a pair o' them 'gator-skin shoes purty bad. The 'gator wuz gettin' tired and ol' Zeke, he hollered at them other guys an' tol' 'em to hep' me git it.

"They saw thet th' 'gator wuz slowin' down, so they poled they pee-row 'long side it, retch'd 'cross it's back, grabbed it' laigs and rolled it over in t' th' boat, with it's laigs in th' air. It wuz still 'live an' wigglin' when Zeke waded up nex' t' 'em. One o' them funny talkin' suckers made a smart-ass r'mark 'bout me an' Zeke wuz stoopid, an' even worse, call'd us Kentuck' boys "*yankees*". Well sir, ol' Zeke, he had his knife 'n his hand. He jist retch'd it right up 'long side th' 'gator's teeth, cut my thin rope, jabbed that ol' 'gator in th' bottom of his tail, an' that damn animal blowed up, like a stick o' dynamite.

"Zeke jumped back in our pee-row, an we got th' hell outtn there, fast as we could push that thang." Gramps took the time to catch his breath and laugh, a little. "Las' time we looked back, them cajuns wus both tryin' t' climb one o' them cypress trees, and that 'gator wuz thrashin' thet boat t' pieces".

Then came the kicker. I'd heard the story before, but this time, Gramps came up with a new ending. "Ya know whut Zeke tol' me on th' way back t' town? He says 'Jake, I was really wantin' me some of those alley-gator shoes, an' after all that trouble we went thru, today, that 'un was barefoot'! HAH!"

My Uncle Ezekiel and Gramps had skinned animals and tanned hides most of their young lives, so Zeke came up with another plan. This one was successful. They set up a store in Houma, with a warehouse in the rear. They paid the locals to bring alligators in, already gutted. They did all the skinning, butchering, and tanning, themselves. Gramps boiled bones, drilled holes in teeth, and made jerky from the meat that didn't sell on the same day of butchering. Zeke traveled as far as New Orleans to sell skins for shoes and purses. Teeth and small bones were sold for jewelry, mostly, but some, along with the larger bones, were sold to a shop that catered to those who practiced voodoo.

Most of the meat, fresh and jerked, was sold locally.

Six years later, those "stupid Kentucky boys" had a bank account of over thirty thousand dollars. One of their nine other employees had been wanting to buy their business, and told them, one day, that he had a banker who was willing to back him. Gramps was 26 and had married Grandma a few months earlier. Zeke, 21, had girlfriends all over Louisiana, but nobody serious. Like I said, Zeke could talk anybody into doing anything, so he and Gramps sold 'Jefferson Brothers' to the man for twenty thousand, took their holdings, and headed west in May, of 1861.

They spent some time in central Texas, but there was talk of a pending war over slavery, and whether the south could pull out and make their own, independent country. As a result, the three of them moved on west to Colorado country. Uncle Zeke saw Little Dove at a trading post and couldn't believe his eyes. She smiled at him, and for the first time in his life, he couldn't talk. He was spellbound by the beauty and grace of an Indian "squaw".

"Damn, Jake", he told gramps later, "did ya see that woman in th' blue skirt? I' tell ya, brother, she was purtier than a speckle' pup, unner a red wagon." Gramps said he hadn't noticed, but he and Grandma, both, saw a twinkle in his eyes, that no girl had ever put there before.

Someway, Zeke and Little Dove got through the language barrier. They courted for a couple of months. Then he gave her father an alligator skin, along with a hand full of 'gator teeth, and Little Dove was his. They all lived in a small mountain cabin for two years, trapping and hunting, then decided to move to California.

Over the years, the men tried gold mining, deep sea fishing, and a few other ventures. Although they made a little money on nearly everything they tried, it was the giant redwoods that set off the bells in Uncle Zeke's head. They quickly set up two, water-driven sawmills, about twenty miles apart. They hired men who knew logging, bought good, strong teams of horses, mules and oxen, and Zeke began checking out markets.

Within three years, 'Jefferson Brothers Redwood' was shipping redwood lumber as far east as Boston, Massachusetts. Thirty years later, with the introduction of gasoline powered engines, the sawmills were converted, and the company was even more productive.

Twelve Ford pickups were ordered in 1914, to transport personnel to and from jobsites. Some Ford Model T trucks were pressed into use in 1918, but, in 1920, Packard introduced a seven ton truck, which could quickly haul many logs to the mills. Uncle Zeke used to brag about his success in persuading James Ward Packard and Henry Ford to travel to California, look at their operation, and build custom trucks for the logging industry.

"Wonder whut's takin' Zeke so long? He ot'ter be gittin' home by now." Gramps observed.

Mom, Dad and I always tried to bring him back to the present when he started thinking like that. "Gramps, Uncle Zeke's been gone three years now, remember? He's buried in the graveyard over there, with his alligator boots on. You remember that?"

"Oh yeah, I 'member, now. Davey boy, will ya do yer ol' Gramps a good favor?"

I knew what was coming next. It was going to be the same, funny joke he always asked, whenever there was any mention of death, burial, etc.

"Sure, Gramps, what's the favor?"

"Well, son, Zeke always did want t' be burry'd in them 'gator skin boots. Friend of ours, in New Orleens, made 'em fer him, back 'n '59. Name was Walter Walters. Kinda funny, huh? Whut I want, when it's my turn t' go, is a good, stout, redwood box, boy. Git it carv'd outten th' heart o' one of them bigun's. Thet way, th' only seam'll be whar th' lid fits. Put my ol' butt in it, face down, but first, fill it plumb up with titties an' I'll be happy thru 'ternity. HAH!"

EPILOGUE

Jacob Jefferson died in 1925 at the age of 91. 80 years later, Jefferson Brothers Redwood continues to be a major producer of redwood lumber.

Jake's son-in-law, my father, Will Baxter, ran the operation for twelve years, and was killed in a logging accident.

I, Dave Baxter, ran the family business for fifty-one years but, in 1988, I turned it over to my sons, Jacob and Ezekiel, and included their cousin, Jefferson Wilson.

Soon, our Board of Directors will be selecting, from the fifth generation, new officers for the company.

The Wagons of Perro Loco

Whiskers pulled the freight wagon into Perro Loco just before dark. It would be morning before Curt, the station agent and half owner of the company, would be back to check-in the load. He drove the Kentucky built, tandem axle, rig to the livery, where it could be secured for the night.

Tandem axle wagons were rare in most of the country, but a common site in places like Perro Loco, a mining town in south central Colorado. Having four rear wheels, two in front of the other two, plus smaller front wheels, the wagon was built, specifically, for hauling very heavy loads.

"Lock 'er up good, Pete," Whiskers told the livery owner, "There's a lot of dynamite on this one. Curt would be madder'n hell if anything should happen to it. Me, too, as far as that goes, we've got a bundle of money tied up here. If anyone should come by looking for me, tell 'em I'll be at the Crazy Dog for a little while, then I'll head on home. Lucy will have supper ready by the time I get there."

"Well, I cain't 'magine who'd be lookin' fer yore sorry ass, Whiskers." Pete countered, "Nobody in their right mind even likes ya, 'cept thet daughter of yore's. Mebbe if she'd run yore stinkin' butt off, she'd find a good man t' take up with her. 'Course they ain't many good men 'round these parts, anyway. In fact, th' onliest good man I kin thank of 'round here, whut ain't awready hitched, is *me*. But li'l Lucy ain't really my type. Too young 'n too purty. Yore poor ol' wife did a helluva good job raisin' thet girl, in spite of her no-good daddy."

"I thank you for those kind words of encouragement, Pete," Whiskers countered, "If you weren't one of my worst enemies, I'd give you a hug. Come t' think of it, I'll give you one anyway, jist for being so sweet."

As Whiskers climbed down, the grizzled old liveryman told him, "You even try t' put them big arms 'round me, I'll stick ya in th' guts with this here pitchfork, smart ass. Then I'll strap ya t' thet load of firecrackers 'n set it on far."

Quick as a snake strike, Carlton 'Whiskers' Long snatched the three pronged pitchfork from Pete's hands and threw it aside. Grinning, he began moving toward the little man, backing him into the wall.

"Damn you, Whiskers, don'cha do it!"

Whiskers wrapped his arms around Pete and told him that it felt nearly as good as hugging one of the girls at Cassie's, the local whore house. "You know Margie, th' skinny, ugly one? Maybe that's why you remind me of her, you being as skinny and ugly as you are. I wonder if you kin kiss as good, too?"

"Put me down, you big son-of-a-bitch!" Pete wailed, "If I ever git loose, I'ma gonna kill ya.!"

Whiskers squeezed a little tighter and whispered close to Pete's ear, "Now you wouldn't do that, would you, darlin'? I guess I'll jist have t' keep on holdin' you tight 'till you decide you like it."

"Awright, awright! I ain't gonna kill ya, jist put my ass down. I need t' git them hosses loose 'n fed . . . . I jist fergot, fer a minute, thet I need ya around t' pay me my wages on Friday."

Whiskers chuckled, released Pete, and ducked a half-hearted punch, thrown by the old timer. As near as anyone could figure, Pete had to be somewhere in his sixties. He was running the stable in Perro Loco long before Whiskers, Curtis Hornsby, and the Bank of Denver established The Longhorn Express Company. Pete had a reputation of being dependable and fair, so when Longhorn purchased that business, also, Pete remained in charge, as a full-time, paid employee. Over the last eight years, the bank note had been paid off, leaving Whiskers and Curt as equal partners.

Curt had the task of running the office and scheduling loads and drivers, all six of them. Whiskers made the most difficult trips, and saw to it that all the wagons were in shape to make any haul at any time. The drivers were well seasoned in handling teams of mules and horses. Whiskers, himself, had selected each one. Not only did they have be able to handle teams, they had to be smart and strong, in order to load freight and load it properly.

Improper weight distribution could cause any number of problems with the wagon, team, or the freight, itself.

Business was very good, in the 1870's. Although rail lines had started to criss-cross the American West, many places still depended on local freight haulers to bring people, and necessities, from the railheads. The majority of their business was traveled on established routes to Denver and Albuquerque, plus the long haul, to Kansas City and back. Most loads were merchandise, which was bought by Longhorn Express, and transported to Perro Loco by Longhorn Express. It was then sold, distributed and hauled to other businesses by . . . . Longhorn Express. Their smallest, and fastest, rigs were used to transport passengers, and an occasional payroll.

Whiskers and Curt were honest men and treated all their customers fairly. They expected to be treated the same. Sixteen businesses became the property of Longhorn Express over the years, as the results of not paying for loads of merchandise. Eight more became partially owned, until the business could get back on it's feet. Their customers knew that Longhorn Express would supply goods at a fair price, but also knew that the bill was to be paid upon delivery.

Neither Curt, nor Whiskers, were interested in running other businesses. The ones they had to take over were quickly sold, usually to a local bank, which had the capital to pay Longhorn, *and* had the time and resources to find another buyer for the business.

"See you in the morning', Pete." whiskers called out, "If Curt gets here before me, don't let him try t' unload anything, with his bad back. If one of th' other men is here, he can do th' heavy work, and Curt can count th' contents. It all needs t' be transferred t' th' warehouse as quick as we can. I should be here by that time."

Whiskers made his way down the street to the Crazy Dog, a saloon named with the English version of the town's Mexican name. He loved this peaceful town. There were two general mercantile stores, a lumber mill, two doctors, two livery stables (other than their own), the best blacksmith within a hundred miles, several other small businesses, the land office, the assay office, four mining company offices, Peterman logging operations office, the Perro Loco News, Cassie's Relaxation Parlor, and the Crazy Dog, the lone surviving saloon in town.

Wick Brandon, the saloon's owner, was a smart and highly respected businessman. He had systematically bought out the town's other three bars, closed them, sold the buildings and consolidated all the business into the Crazy Dog.

"Howdy, Whiskers," the bartender, spoke up, "rye and a beer this evenin'?"

"Sounds good, Nate" he replied, "th' boss around?"

"Yep, but he's gone out back ta th' privy. If he ever falls in, we won't know how much shit ta dip out. It'll all look th' same."

Whiskers chuckled and said, "Good one, Nate. When he does come back in, tell him I need t' see him. I'll be in th' other room, ok?"

"Sure, I'll tell 'im. Don' mean he gonna hear me, though. I swear thet man don' hear me haf 'th time. Or mebbe he jist got so much goin' on in thet thick head, he don' lissen ta a dumb-ass ol' bartender, no more. But, I'll tell 'im."

"Excuse me, old timer," a tall young man spoke to Whiskers as he walked into the adjoining room, "you're not allowed to wear your sidearm in this saloon. You'll need to go back and check it in at the bar."

Whiskers knew everyone in town and this stranger was new to him. What a perfect opportunity to have a little fun.

"Whutzzat, sonny?" he asked, as he leaned a little closer, pretending to be hard of hearing.

"I said, you will have to check your gun at the bar!" the man answered a little louder.

Whiskers was raising his own voice, now, just inches from the stranger's ear. "Yer gonna have ta speak up, sonny. I cain't hear too good. I use'ta be married t' a loud mouth woman, 'n she plumb wore out my pore ol' ears. Ya got t' purty much holler in my face 'n talk kinda slow, so's I kin read yer lips, too!"

The crowd in the saloon had turned their attention to the loud discussion going on near the doorway. Most of the patrons already knew Whiskers, and were fully aware of his boast of 'being able to hear a gnat piss, a quarter-mile away.'

As the young man looked into the older one's eyes, he opened his mouth wide and began to speak loud and slow, so Whiskers could read his lips.

Whiskers eased his Colt Army single action from his holster and waited for the man to say 'bar', at the end of his statement.

"You mean this here gun, sonny?" Whiskers asked as he quickly stuck the barrel into the man's mouth, with his right hand, and grabbed the back of his head with his left, making it impossible for him to draw away from his sudden predicament.

The poor stranger nearly fainted, and nodded his head, slightly. "Yeth, thir." he mumbled.

Whiskers smiled at the stranger, removed the pistol from his mouth and said, calmly and quietly, "Here, sonny, would you please be kind enough t' take this t' Nate? You won't need t' tell him who it belongs to, he's seen it a hundred times. Besides, he and twenty more men have just seen you make an ass outta yourself."

As the man laid the gun on the bar, Nate told him, "You is one lucky sumbitch, stranger. I been knowin' thet man fer more'n five y'ars, 'n ain't nobody never tetched thet gun. It's a wonder ya ain't layin' in yonder with a hole in yer purty haid. He wuz funnin' with ya, but jist 'member this, pardner, don' never make th' mistake o' makin' Whiskers Long mad. If'n he'd ever cocked thet pistol, you'da been in deep shit, mister. Ya ain't never seen a hair trigger like this'un here's got."

"I wasn't trying to start anything, Nate, I had to check my own gun. I didn't know who that old feller was, and I didn't want him to get in trouble for wearing one."

Nate carefully placed the Colt on the rack under the bar and called to the stranger, as he was walking away. "That 'old feller', as you jist called him, is Whiskers Long, half owner of Longhorn Express Company, he's a damn good man. Ya would prob'ly be smart t' git yer ass back in thar 'n 'pologize t' Whiskers, mister."

Wick Brandon had joined Whiskers at a table near the stage. There was no entertainment scheduled for that evening, but everyone present had already seen a good show. In fact, the saloon owner and the teamster were discussing the incident when the young man walked up to their table.

Whiskers cupped his hand behind his ear and raised his voice, "What'cha need, sonny? Speak up now!"

The man took a deep breath and yelled, loud enough for everyone in the bar to hear, "I want to apologize, Mr. Long. It wasn't my place to say anything about you wearing your side arm. I'm sorry, sir."

He extended his hand and Whiskers took it. "That took balls, mister." Whiskers said. "You're a better man than first impressions might indicate. But, jist call me Whiskers, *Mr. Long* was my grand pappy."

The stranger then turned to Wick Brandon, "I apologize to you also, sir. What goes on in here is your business, not mine."

They shook hands and Wick spoke, "No problem young man, but, just for the record, Whiskers is one of only four men allowed to pack a firearm in here. Myself and two lawmen are the other three. Now, seeing as how you're big enough to apologize, let me buy you a drink. This thing is over and done, right, Whiskers?"

The man thanked Wick for the offer, but declined the drink. "I already had one beer, to cut the dust from my throat. I never have more than one a day. I've seen what too much drink can do to a man, and I never want to be there. Thanks again."

Whiskers asked the interesting man to be seated. He introduced himself as Augustus MacKenzie. "Just call me Mack, please." Mack had come from Kansas, looking for work as a wrangler on a horse ranch. "Horses are amazing animals and I like working with them, especially teams of draft animals. If you know of any ranches hiring, I'd appreciate knowing who to talk to."

Whiskers asked Mack if he could handle a six-horse hitch. "I can handle an eight, easily, and back home, I trained a ten-horse. Before I die, I want to see one of those twenty mule teams I've heard about, that haul some kind of powder out of Death Valley, in California. That's gotta be a sight to see."

"Can you lift a hundred pounds?" Whiskers asked. He had a gut feeling about this man, and his gut had a pretty record. His business was thriving, and he had been thinking about starting a freight route to, and from, Amarillo, Texas. This good-looking, powerfully built young man might be an asset to his pool of drivers.

"I can lift you, sir, and you have to be over two hundred, possibly two-twenty. I'd rather not do that, though. I'm thinking, I've been too close to you one time too many, already."

All three men laughed, and Whiskers asked Mack to come home with him for supper. "My daughter always cooks more than we need, so there'll be plenty for you, if you're hungry. Besides, I may know of a job for you, unless Wick needs you here, t' disarm the customers."

Mack grinned and admitted that he could use a good meal. "I've still got enough cash for a hotel room, for a few days, and enough to eat on. But, the quicker I can find work, the better. I don't mind taking a few days off, from time to time, but I like to work. And one thing's for sure, Mr. Lon . . . I mean, Whiskers, I ain't never been stupid enough to pass up a home cooked meal. I 'preciate the invite."

"It always amazes me, how you always know when I'm taking supper off the stove." nineteen year-old Lucille Long set a cast-iron pot on the, two inch thick, red oak dining table, and turned to her father. "This chicken, cheese, and dumpling casserole just came out of the oven. Who's your friend?"

"This here is Mr. Augustus MacKenzie, but he prefers t' be called Mack. You got 'nuff supper for him, too?"

"Well," she replied, smiling, "With the creamed corn, boiled new potatos, the spinach salad, and some biscuits left over from breakfast, we'll try to make it stretch. Your hands are dirty. Go on out to the porch and wash up, you, too, Mr. Mack. Everything will be on the table when you two get back."

Lucy was fifteen when her mother died during childbirth. The child was stillborn, also, and Lucy had been the woman of the house since. She had developed into a fine cook and an immaculate housekeeper. She knew how much her father liked to 'show her off' and brag on her, so she was never surprised when he brought someone home for supper.

Whiskers was, indeed, proud of Lucy. She was the most precious thing in his life, and he would do anything, within his power, to make her happy. And . . . . the thing that made *her* happiest was her father's love. Although, at times, he tried her patience. Like trying to do some matchmaking with Curt's son, Brody Hornsby.

Brody was a good friend, and had been since he and Lucy were eight years old. Even though Brody had an interest in the local school teacher, Millie White, Whiskers kept trying to get Lucy to pay him more attention.

Brody working as a foreman for Peterman Logging. He worked hard and was a quick learner. The men, who worked under his supervision, respected him, his fairness and his judgment. When any of them disagreed with him on a work issue, he was quick to consider the other man's opinion, with an open mind. Production and safety, both, improved as a result of many compromises.

He, also, considered Lucy as a good friend, and was content with that relationship.

"Would you like some coffee, Mr. Mack?" Lucy's blue eyes were looking directly into the tall young man's brown ones. "It's my own blend."

"It's th' best you can ever find in these here parts, too, Mack." Whiskers boasted. "Lucy parches cornmeal, acorns, and something else. Then she grinds 'em up, mixes it with two pounds of Arbuckle's dark roast, and adds an egg, t' a pot full. I ain't real sure which part makes it taste so damn good, but it's th' best you'll ever drink."

"Thank you, miss Lucy, I usually don't drink anything but water this late in the day, but with your father's sales pitch, I'm looking forward to a cup full." Mack couldn't help but admire the beauty of the woman. "But, just one cup, please. If I drink too much, the slop jar, in my hotel room, won't be big enough to hold all I'll have to drain tonight."

"Oh no!" Mack thought to himself, *"I can't believe I'm talking to a beautiful woman about pissing in a slop jar. Stupid! Stupid! Stupid!"*

Whiskers laughed as he saw the young man start squirming.

Lucy just smiled bigger and said, "One cup it is, then, sir."

Mack decided that this was the best meal he had ever eaten. Maybe it was the casserole, maybe the coffee, of which he had two refills. Maybe it was the job offer Whiskers made him. But, definitely, the smiling face across the table from him was the biggest factor.

Whiskers talked through the whole meal. Something about a load of rocks, Amarillo, Texas, the big wagon, a ten-day trip, etc.

"Say!" he said as he tapped Mack on the shoulder, "Are you hearing me?" He had noticed the attraction between Mack and Lucy, and thought neither was paying attention to what he was saying.

"Yes sir," Mack replied, "I heard every word. You said that you wanted me and Bob to go to Amarillo with you, on the tandem wagon. You're hauling a load of slab rocks, marble I think, to the undertaker there. It'll be a ten-day trip. You want to take an extra team, because the load is heavy and it'll reduce down time, for resting the mules."

"Well I'll be damned, you did hear me."

"Daddy, watch your language in front of company." Lucy chastised.

"Sorry, baby girl," he replied, "I didn't think either of you was listenin'."

"These two are moony-eyed over each other." he thought, *"I hope Brody doesn't get wind of this and kick this boy's ass. Looking at his arms, though, Brody might jist have his hands full."*

"Well, we might as well let Mack get t' his bed. If he's gonna help unload that dynamite wagon in the morning, he's gonna need some rest. 'Course, when I was his age, I never needed any rest." Whiskers then lapsed into a tale of working 32 hour days, courting six women at the same time, keeping the town safe, in the capacity of a lawman, and supplying his parents with food and game. "Yep, I was a busy boy. Sometimes I'd go six or eight months without sleep. But times have changed and you pups, today, need rest.

"So Lucy and me'll say goodnight t' you, Mack. I'll see you at 'bout six in th' morning. Come ready t' work hard. I'd like t' get th' wagon ready t' head out by Friday, if th' rock will be ready by then."

Mack thanked them for the meal, and the job. He couldn't wait for the next opportunity to see Lucy, again.

The big wagon rumbled along, through the heat of the Texas Panhandle. One more day, and they'd be in Amarillo.

"At least this trip is being made in late September," Mack thought, *"During July or August, I'll bet hell would be cooler than this place. I'll be glad to get back to Colorado, next week. I hope I see Lucy again, too. It sounds to me like the guy Whiskers wants her to be interested in, must be alright. I just hope she's not interested in him.*

"What am I thinking about, I got no right to think she'd be interested in me. I got nothing but this job and my two horses. That Brody fella is a foreman at the loggin' company, plus he's probably gonna own the express company, someday. It'll take all I make to feed me and my horses. I'm gettin' along fine with her paw and Bob, but I gotta let her know I'm interested in her, though. It may be a wasted effort, but I ain't never known a woman like her."

"Ya day dreamin' or sumthin'? Bob asked. He and Mack were on the wagon. Whiskers was wrangling the extra mules and horses. They all three had been rotating driving, wrangling and resting. "Ya ain't said a word fer th' last half-hour."

"Naw, Bob, I've just been thinkin' about what the future will bring. I'm not sure I can make enough money hauling rocks." he snickered and pointed his thumb back toward the heavily loaded wagon. "'specially tombstone material. I could see making good money hauling gold ore, even silver, but not marble.

"Someday I want to be able to get a wife, kids and a small horse ranch. I don't think I can do it on a teamster's pay."

"Ya jist cain't never tell, Mack, Whiskers an' Curt didn't have nuthin when they started out. But ever'body knew they was honest, an' worked hard. Me an' th' other drivers make a decent living, an' three of them is hitched. 'Blue' even has five kids, an' all them is fat an' sassy. 'Course his woman is purty big, too. 'Blue' says he gets his boy to brang little pieces of chalk home from school. He keeps a piece of it in his pocket, all'a time. Says when he hugs his woman, he takes thet chalk, marks as fer as he kin reach, then goes 'round, starts at th' mark an' hugs th' rest of her." Bob chuckled and continued, "thing is, he tells thet story right in front of her. She jist shakes her finger at him an' grins."

"I guess I ain't met Blue, yet," Mack said, "Sounds like he's quite a character."

"All us Longhorn drivers gotta stay on our toes. The one thet comes up with th' best story gets a real treat, come the end of th' month. Th' winner gits t' go t' Cassie's an' pick out th' girl he wants. Th' bosses do th' payin' an' we do th' playin'. We all had t' take a vote, though. Cain't nobody top all th' bullshit Whiskers comes up with, so we voted his ass out of th' com . . . . th' comp . . . . th' . . . ."

"The competition?" Mack helped get the word out of Bob.

"Yeah, thet's it. Hell, he was beatin' all of us ever' month. He makes a reg'lur trip over there, anyways, so he was savin' money ever' time he won th' com . . . , well, hell, ever' time he won."

Mack was laughing when Whiskers rode up beside the wagon.

"Get your rifle ready, Mack," he said quietly, "We got Comanches ahead. They ain't been bad, lately, but when they stop us, let me do th' talkin'. Don't shoot anyone, unless I start it. Jist be ready t' take as many of 'em down as you can, if we have to."

Four Indians rode in to block the trail. Their regalia was a rainbow of colors. Blacks, reds, yellows, white and orange . . . Breastplates made of bone, laced with colorful beads . . . Leggings, fully beaded to match the designs on their moccasins . . . Dangling feathers and dyed horse hair, woven into the manes of their mounts, gave the impression of a high-ranking delegation, rather than a party of warriors or hunters. Semi-circles of multi-color beads, dropped from the tops of the men's noses, crossed the top of the cheek bones, and raised back to their temples. The black paint, within those circles, around their eyes, fascinated Mack.

"I've never seen Indians dressed as fancy as these," Mack spoke softly to Bob, "I'm impressed."

"They only dress up like this t' rob a load of rocks." Bob said, "it's sumthin' special fer 'em. Ya don't git many loads of marble on this here trail."

It was all Mack could do to keep from laughing out loud. "That's gotta be one for the competition this month. I don't think I can top it."

Whiskers rode along side, again, just as the wagon came to a stop. He told Mack to watch the stock, and be very visible with his rifle. He then rode, slowly, to meet the Comanche delegation.

After a few minutes discussion, he returned, told Mack to cut out the worst two mules, and lead them to the Indians. He dismounted, pulled two sacks of coffee from under the wagon seat, and handed them to Mack, as he was walking the mules past the wagon, toward the Indians.

"Give me your rifle, sonny. As soon as they take th' coffee, jist let th' mules go, and stand with your hand on your pistol. Don't move fast, but don't show 'em you're about t' shit your pants, either. They *should* jist take th' mules and haul ass outta here. Leastways, that's what they said they'd do."

Mack did what he was told and the Comanches left, without further ado. He admired the skill with which they handled their horses. Only the man leading the mules had his horse's rein in his other hand. The others rode hands-free, controlling their tri-colored paints with touches from their knees or toes.

"I've got to know how the Comanches do that", Mack thought, *"I can train my horses to respond to some knee commands, but they make look so easy.*

"I'll have to get one of them to show me how it's done. Wonder how I can make that happen? If Bob doesn't know, I'll bet Whiskers does."

"Well, sonny, what do ya think of your first meetin' with Indians?" Whiskers asked as Mack was still standing, watching the riders disappear over a small rise. "Was you scared?"

"Actually, I wasn't." he replied, "in fact, I'd really like to know them better. They ride as good as any man I've known, and I'd like to find out how they do it. You already know I'm pretty damn good with horses, but I'm not as good as they are."

Whiskers told his men that the Indians were on a trading mission. Quite frankly, their people were hungry. Whiskers, being a resourceful businessman, gave the mules to them, with an agreement of no interference with his freight wagons. The coffee was an extra, which wasn't negotiated. "Never hurts t' put a little icing on th' cake, even if th' cake don't need it.

"You mount up, now, I'll drive a while and let Bob rest, fer a little bit. We're short two mules, now, so we're gonna have t' start rotating what we have left. You figure out th' rotation, and how often we'll do it. This load needs a full team."

"No problem, boss," Mack said, "three of them are good lead mules. As long as we keep one of them up front, we won't have any trouble working the others in. as long as we're stopped, we might as well make the first change now."

As the tandem stopped, inside the Amarillo livery barn, six men with badges entered, through the rear door. Whiskers greeted the town marshal, and instructed Mack, and Bob, to lift the slab of blue tint marble. It was directly in the center of the load, so there was a question, in Mack's mind, . . . why start in the middle?

He soon found out the reason, as he and Bob tilted the stone up. Most of the marble was eight inches thick, but this one was much thinner, two inches. Underneath was a layer of one inch boards, under which was a locked strongbox. The marshal handed Whiskers a key, which he used to unlock two padlocks. When the lid was raised, Mack's eyes widened as he saw the gold bullion, inside.

He looked at Whiskers and started to speak. . . . "I'll explain it t' you, later, sonny," Whiskers spoke first, "right now though, we need t' step back and let these boys do what they're getting' paid t' do."

The deputies unloaded the gold into a small, stout wagon, pulled by two beautiful, strong Morgan horses. Everyone waited, for a short time, until dark.

When the marshal and his heavily armed escort left, Whiskers explained that they had just brought seven hundred thousand dollars, in gold, to the Ranchers Bank of Amarillo. Although Bob was aware of the main reason to haul 'rocks' to Texas, Whiskers had decided not to say anything to Mack, until he felt that he could trust the new man.

"Well, sonny," he addressed Mack, "I think you're an honest man. Th' more I'm around ya, th' more I'm convinced of it. I'm sure I kin trust ya, now. We don't make a high-paying trip like this very often. When Curt came up with th' idea of hiding th' gold under all that stone, it didn't take much t' convince th' mine owners. After all, who wants t' risk prison, or their lives, by robbing a load of tombstones, not me. Oh yeah, there was a twenty man escort, just two miles behind us. The mine owners sent some 'insurance' with us. When we arrived, they came on in. Right now they're at th' bank. More 'insurance.'

"Th' gold will be in th' vault in a few minutes. Th' city leaders will have a crew here in th' morning, t' unload th' rocks, for th' cemetery. We should have a load of cow hides for our back-haul, and we'll leave about th' middle of th' afternoon. Mack, I want ya t' find two more good mules. We'll do some night traveling on th' way home. There's a dance on Saturday, and I got a date."

"I got a question, sir," Mack spoke quietly, "Did you just say *seven . . . hundred . . . thousand . . . God . . . damned . . . dollars?* That comes closer to making me shit my pants than the Comanches did!"

Whiskers and Bob laughed and told Mack that he now had a story for the competition this month.

The three travelers headed for the Cattlemen's, a nearby hotel, which had excellent dining, a large bathhouse, and a saloon.

After Mack had his beer, his bath, and the biggest steak supper he'd ever seen, he bid good-night to the other two and went to bed. *"If that guy, Brody, hasn't already asked Lucy to that dance, I'm going to, just as soon as I get back to Perro Loco."* he thought as he was slipping into his dreams.

Mack couldn't wait. At 5:30 the next morning, he was at the telegraph office. The wire read, *To: Miss Lucille Long . . . stop . . . Perro Loco, Colorado . . . stop . . . leaving Amarillo tomorrow . . . stop . . . I request the pleasure of your company for dance Saturday night . . . stop . . . answer asap please . . . stop . . . A. MacKenzie.*

At nine a.m., Mack checked with the key operator, . . . for the fourth time. This time his return wire had arrived. *To: Mr. A. Mackenzie . . . stop . . . have a date already . . . stop . . . you may know him . . . stop . . . name Mr. Mack . . . stop . . . have good trip . . . stop . . . L.Long.*

The telegraph operator, who was listening to his key and transcribing another message, jumped when Mack let out a whoop and ran from the office. "Damn kid," he mumbled, "now I don't know if that word was 'where' or 'whore'. I believe 'where' is gonna fit better on this one."

"Well, sonny," Whiskers said to Mack as they were leaving Pete's Livery, "You got plans for tonight? If you don't, there's always th' dance at th' schoolhouse. Starts at seven. Bet'cha you can meet some gals there, if you're interested."

"Actually, boss, I've already got a date for the dance." Mack patted him on the shoulder and turned, "see ya there."

Whiskers stopped and watched as the twenty-three year old walked off. After thinking for a minute, it dawned on him, *"Wait a minute . . . . he's only met one girl since he's been in this here town . . . . Lucy. Who in th' hell could he have a date with? She'll be going with Bro . . . . Oh, hell. Brody's got competition. Well, at least Mack's a good man. Brody's going t' be pissed off, though. I better keep an eye on 'em tonight."*

Everyone in Perro Loco was at the dance. The schoolyard was full of people. The food was laid out on tables, inside the school house. The fiddles, guitars, banjo, and harmonica players were doing what they loved to do. The children ran in and out, grabbing food and chasing each other. Parents felt comfortable that their children were safe and let them have their fun.

Several men, who usually were prone to too much drink, were on good behavior. The town's two lawmen were constantly circling in and out of the crowd, being visible, friendly and tolerant.

Lucy had her left arm looped through Mack's right, as they stepped into the dance area. She was surprised at Mack's dancing ability. He explained that his two big sisters always had to have someone to practice with, in his younger years.

"Well then, I like your sisters already," she smiled and continued, "How in the world will they make it, now, without you for a practice partner?"

The smile left Mack's face and he became serious, "They both died, Lucy, but can we talk about that some other time? I just want to have fun tonight . . . . with you."

Lucy's mouth dropped, and she apologized to Mack.

"No, it's alright, Lucy, you had no idea. I'll tell you the whole story later."

The music changed to a slow waltz, Mack put his arm around her and pulled her a little closer. There was only he and Miss Lucy Long in the whole world, right now. He saw the dimples, the smile, the wisp of blonde hair that kept falling across her cheek, and the tear in her big, beautiful blue eye.

"Hey there, sonny," Whiskers' loud voice broke through the air, "You might outta loosen up on that waist." he was staring straight into Mack's eyes. "Sometimes she bruises easy. I don't like it when my girl gets hurt. Besides, when Brody Hornsby gets here, you may just need all th' strength you can muster."

Mack stopped, turned Lucy loose and faced Whiskers, "Mister Long, sir, there's no way I would hurt you daughter, in any way. You might as well get used to me being around, because, as long as she's ok with it, I'm going to be around . . . . every chance I get.

"If that doesn't set well with Brody, then he and myself will handle it. There's no need for you to be concerned. Now, sir, I'd like to dance with my date."

Mack turned, took Lucy's hand and joined the other dancers in the Virginia Reel, just as it was finishing up.

She smiled at her escort and said, "Wow, I've never seen anyone stand up to my father like that, without getting a broken nose. I think he was impressed, too, he's still standing there looking at us. No, now he's asking Cassie to dance. Good job, Mr. Mack." "Oh! I want you to meet someone." She led Mack to a handsome young couple, just joining the party, "Brody!" she gave the young man a quick hug, "This is Mr. Mack, he's my date, tonight. He dances better than you, too. Hi Millie!"

Lucy introduced Millicent White to Mack, explained that she was the school teacher, and that she and Brody had been seeing each other for a few weeks.

Brody told them that he had just asked Millie to marry him . . . she said 'yes'.

"Daddy was afraid you'd be mad about me being with Mr. Mack, tonight. I've been telling him that you and I are just friends, but he kept thinking we'd get together. I'm so happy for you and Millie."

"I'm pleased to meet you, Mr. MacKenzie, I've heard Whiskers and my dad talk about you. I know this much, Lucy's been my best friend since we were little kids. I trust her judgment. If she says you're ok, then you're alright with me." The two men shook hands, and Brody added, "Now, I came to eat and dance with my bride-to-be. Let's get started."

Dawn, on Monday morning, found Lucy in the kitchen, fixing breakfast for her father and Curt, and daydreaming about the goodnight kiss Mack had given her, after the dance. He would be away until next Sunday, hauling lumber to western Kansas, and returning with a load of feed corn.

"If I make good time," he had told Lucy, "I'm going to ride on over to see my mother. It'll be Thursday before I can get started back, so I should have enough time to make a quick trip. She's close to fifty, now, and it's been nearly a year since I've seen her. Curt paid me a bonus for the load of 'rocks' we took to Amarillo, and I'll leave that money with her. Maybe, once I know for sure that I'll be staying here in Perro Loco, I'll just move her out here. What would you think about that?"

"That other pot ready, yet, honey?" Whiskers called out to Lucy. "These cups are gettin' cold as ol' Jughead's wet nose."

"Yep, Daddy, I just put the egg in it. You need some more, too, Curt?"

That pot of coffee, and one more, was emptied before the partners headed for the office. The logging company had just ordered transportation for two hundred loads of lumber, to the railhead in Denver, where rail cars would haul it back east. Winter would be setting in before long, and every trip needed to be scheduled, as soon as possible.

"We'll need to put on ten extra drivers, and get three more wagons." Curt explained, "None of them will get any time off, until the mountain passes get blocked. With any luck, we'll have more than half the lumber shipped by then. After that, we'll have to make the long haul, to Kansas City. We won't do back-haul loads on every other trip. That will take a full day off each of those runs."

"I'm gonna talk t' Mack, soon's he gets back from Kansas, about that ten-horse hitch." Whiskers told Curt, "If it don't take a lot, we'll even use th' two tandems. With that much pull, we can use horses instead of mules. It'll be a little faster, an' we won't have t' change teams as often. Bob an' Webfoot should be able t' handle a team that size.

"Until Mack gets back, we'll get Charlie t' take six teams of mules, an' ten horses t' Pueblo. When a change is needed, they'll be there. I'll make sure Pete an' Bones (the blacksmith) are on th' ball, getting th' wagons and harness in shape. Right now, I've gotta find more drivers. As soon as th' men start showing up, send them to th' mill. We might as well get a jump on this job. Charlie needs to get that stock t' Pueblo right away, too."

Whiskers hired three teen age boys to help Charlie, and told them to report to the office as soon as they could get their gear together. If they proved themselves, there would be more work for them, possibly throughout the winter.

Bones knew where three good wagons were available, and Whiskers instructed him to acquire them, and get them ready to haul lumber as soon as possible.

Pete sent one of his grandsons to three ranchers in the area, to inform them that Longhorn Express needed sixty more good mules and horses, right away. "Tell 'em I say'd don' brang no dogs. Don' nobody know good animals better'n me. Tell 'em t' brang me the bes' stock they got. They gonna git paid good."

At the Crazy Dog, Whiskers found six men who seemed acceptable as drivers. *"That'll be enough t' get this started,"* he thought, *"I'll have a couple more days t' find four more."*

Returning home, Whiskers sat Lucy down to explain what was going on. He would take the first load, himself, to Denver. "That way I can make sure things on that end will be ready. I'll have t' rent a warehouse, and hire a crew t' unload our wagons. Th' only thing I want our drivers t' do, is drive. That'll be hard enough on any man for th' next month, t' six weeks. Banking and hotel rooms will have t' be arranged. If th' telegraph wire stays in operation, Curt can handle a purty good bunch of that from here. I'll be runnin' empty on my return trips, so I'll be here every five or six days.

"Now then, young lady, here's th' most important thing. This job, th' business, th' men, th' excitement and work . . . . none of it means as much t' me as you do. I need t' be sure you're ok with . . . you know who. I seen you two at th' dance, and on th' front porch afterwards. You like Mack a lot, don't you?"

"I figured you were watching us Saturday night. Yes, I do like Mack, a lot. In fact, you're the only man I like more. The Lord, only, knows why that is!" she smiled, stood and hugged her father. "I love you, Daddy. Don't you be too concerned about Mack and me, you're going to be keeping him on the road for the next two or three months. I won't be able to see him, anyway. But, I really do like him, Daddy, he may just be your son-in-law someday, if he'll have me.

"But, right now, you need to get this big job up and running. When Mack gets back, Sunday, I'll have a word with him. If something is going to happen between the two of us, we'll all still be here when this job is finished."

"If he'll have you?" Whiskers responded, "That boy would be th' biggest dumb-ass west of th' Mississip' if he'd pass up a woman like my Lucy." Lucy took note . . . . it was the first time her father had ever called her a 'woman'. He had always referred to her as being a 'girl'.

"Now," Whiskers continued, "I gotta be honest with you, honey, I like Mack, myself. I'm convinced he's a good man, with good ways, and good judgment. I guess I'm tryin' t' say I got nothin' against him. If things work out for th' two of you, fine. We haven't known him long, though, so you jist go slow, ok, honey?"

"That's fine, Daddy," Lucy said, teasingly, "I'll try not to let the Long blood get the best of me. If I did, I'd probably be working at Cassie's by now."

"Dammit, Lucille Long, you ain't too big t' git your butt busted." Whiskers stood, shaking his finger at his grinning daughter, "Don't you be pickin' on me or I'll haul you t' th' woodshed. My ol' paddle is still out there an' I ain't forgot how t' use it."

Lucy had been threatened many times, with the paddle in the woodshed, but Whiskers had never touched her with it. As a youngster, a slap on the hand or a swat on the backside was the harshest punishment she ever experienced. Even then, it was the surprise, rather than the pain, which taught her the error of her ways.

"Mack did tell me that he would like to bring his mother to live here, so he can watch after her." Lucy said, "If you don't mind, I'd like to invite her to stay with us, until he can find a place of his own. She's the only one left in Kansas. Something bad happened, but he hasn't opened up about it, yet. Ok if she comes here, Daddy?"

Whiskers told Lucy to do whatever she liked. He trusted her judgment completely, and knew she'd make changes if things didn't work out. He gathered his gear, along with the food Lucy packed for him, kissed her on the cheek and left for Denver.

"So, what do you think, Mr. Mack?" Lucy had just told him about inviting his mother to come stay with her and Whiskers. "She will be comfortable here, and you'll have two women, in the same house, to pay you some attention when you come by."

"You're sure it's alright with your paw?" Mack asked, "I think he might get jealous. He sure likes your attention for himself. I can't blame him, though," he took Lucy's hand and pulled her closer, "One of these days, I'll have a woman, just like you, all to myself. I won't want to share her attention, either."

"Why, Mr. Mack," she was acting a little 'put out' by his statement, "I don't understand. Are you saying you want a woman *like* me, or are you saying you want *me*? If I wanted *you*, for example, I wouldn't say 'I want a man *like* you.'" Lucy snuggled her body against Mack's chest, looked up into his eyes and continued, "You do confuse me, Mr. Mack."

"You be very careful, Lucy Long, I might just kiss you right here on your front porch." Mack put his arms around her, "Just think of all the people that will see us. They'll tell Whiskers, he'll get mad and whip my butt, up and down the street. Then I'll lose my job, and be a disgrace to the whole town. Maybe we'll both be a disgrace. Or would that be 'disgraces'? But, then again, he might be happy. He could just make me marry you, then I'll be the one to have to put up with your sassy britches." His eyes locked onto hers, he smiled and said, "Oh yeah, if that did happen, would you marry me?"

"Are you asking me to marry you, Mr. Mack?" she asked, "Or are you asking, would I, *if* he insisted you marry me?"

"Dammit, woman, now who's confusing who?" He pulled her up and kissed her soundly, "It's either you, or a woman like you. I'm bettin' the Lord didn't make two alike, so . . . . Will you marry me, Lucy? I'm going to be so busy for the next three months, I need to know now, so I can either be happy, or get over it, depending on your answer."

She reached her arms around his neck, "Why would you want to marry me, Mr. Mack?" before he could answer she stretched up and kissed him, again.

As she backed down, grinning at Mack, he said, "Several reasons I can think of, first, . . . you make the best coffee a man could ever drink. Second, . . . you're a really good dancer. Third, . . . I need a place for my mother to live, for a while. . . . Fourth," he kissed her again, "There's no telling what stories are going to be told, with the show we're putting on for the neighbors. And fifth, . . . as smart as you are, I figger you're just dumb enough to say 'yes' to a poor ol' wrangler, with a soft spot for a spoiled woman. Oh yes, I just about forgot . . . . I love you, Lucille Long, and I will forever."

Her smile was so big that her teeth hurt, "Yep, I guess you're right, I'm just dumb enough to say 'yes'. I guess I'll marry you, Augustus MacKenzie. Since Millie hooked Brody, there's nobody else around worth having. I'll just settle for you, Mr. Mack, for the rest of our lives . . . . Oh yes, I just about forgot, I love you, too."

Mack's meeting with Curt produced an unexpected surprise. He and Bob were to take the two big wagons, with eight-horse hitches, to the railhead in Kansas City with big loads of six-inch thick lumber. They were to look for three good locations to serve as 'way stations' along the route. As soon as the first snows closed the passes, on the Denver route, the rest of the lumber shipments would use the 'K.C.' route.

Curt had quickly gained confidence in Mack's ability to handle business related situations. "You two will have a total of five thousand dollars with you." he told the men. "Hide most of it wherever you think it will be safe. Never carry more than a few dollars with you at any time. Make arrangements for teams, harness, man power, whatever is needed, so things will be ready when all the drivers have to start making that trip. We'll need a warehouse in K.C, also.

"With the exception of Whiskers, I think you boys are the best ones to take care of this. Don't worry about collecting payment on the other end, just wire me when it's delivered, and I'll do the rest from here. Check the telegraph office as soon as you get the wagons empty, because I'll try to find us some return loads."

"Will it be alright for me to swing down and load up my mother on the way back?" Mack asked, "She'll be staying with Lucy until we get married."

"Married!?" Curt and Bob exclaimed at the same time, "Boy, you don't waste any time, do you?" Curt said, "Does Whiskers know about this, yet?"

Mack explained that the decision was made only a few hours ago, and Lucy would tell her father when he made his return trip, from Denver.

"It'll only add about four hours to the travel time." Mack said, "You can take it out of my pay, and her things won't add much weight to whatever load I'm carrying. I really need to get her moved before winter, Curt, but if you say 'no', I'll understand and work it out later."

Curt approved Mack's request and as the two men were stepping out to the office's porch, Brody ran towards them, with Lucy close behind.

"Something's wrong, Mack," Brody's voice was shaking, "I can't find Millie. One of the kids told Lucy that two men put her in a wagon, and drove west, toward Ash Creek. I'm looking for help. Can you go, or do you need to get your load rolling?"

"You'll have to fill me in on the area, Brody, I'm still not real familiar with most of this country, but I'm a fair hand at tracking."

Curt called out to them, "Take Bob and Webfoot with you. Those loads can wait a little while."

The four men went to the schoolyard, where the youngster had last seen Millie. Mack and Webfoot, both, noticed where one of the steel wagon wheels had left an impression, showing a crack.

The trail was easy to follow for a while, but when the road widened and got rockier, it was a challenge to spot the right track.

"If I find out Blackie Ware did this," Brody was talking to Bob, "I'll kill the bastard. Millie told him months ago that she didn't want to see him. He'd been pestering her, anyway, until I started seeing her a couple months ago. I made it very plain that if he didn't leave her alone, I'd clean the streets of Perro Loco with his ass."

It was hard to keep Brody from barreling ahead, but Mack convinced him to be patient, and let them follow the tracks. With more traffic, the more sign would be destroyed.

Seven or eight miles from town, Webfoot spotted a track leaving the road. "Lookie here at this'un, Mack, see th' dent? I'm purty sure this is th' one."

About ten feet further, Mack confirmed Webfoot's suspicion, finding a clearer sign where the wheel left its next mark. After about another mile, the men heard a woman's scream. None of the other horses could keep up with the short sprint Mack's horse made.

As he rode up on the scene, one of the men turned and looked up, just in time to catch Mack's boot in the face. Mack never slowed his mount as he left the saddle, landing on top of the other man, who was raising his body up, off Millie.

Brody, Bob and Webfoot rode in, as the first man was getting up, just in time to catch a rifle stock in his blind and bleeding face.

Seeing Millie's torn and bloody clothes, Brody easily lifted the two hundred and ten pound Mack, off Blackie Ware, who was already pleading for mercy.

"I warned you, you son-of-bitch!" Brody stated calmly, "you should have listened. Now, you'll see your old man in hell."

Mack yelled for Brody to wait, but it was too late. The big left fist caught Blackie in the front of his throat. His windpipe was crushed. Brody knew he'd done all that was necessary. He dropped the man, kicking and squirming, on the ground, and lifted Millie tenderly.

She wrapped her arms around him, shaking violently.

"Leave us for a while, fellas, ok?" he asked the other three men. With a nod from Mack's head, Bob understood the unspoken message. He looped his rope around the chest of Blackie's friend, Wills Boren.

"Y'all cain't hang me!" he was whining, "I ain't never tetched thet screamin' bitch! It wuz Blackie! All's I ev'r did, wuz hep him ketch her. She a hellcat. Bit his fanger plumb off." Bob told Wills to shut his mouth, but he kept babbling, as he was being pulled further away, "I'm talein' ya, ya cain't hang me! It's 'ginst th' law!"

Mack, who had been walking behind the rest, kicked Wills' feet backward, tripping the man. As soon as he hit the ground, Mack's boot crushed his nose. "Bob told you to shut your mouth, dumbass, it's only gonna take one, just one, more word for me to cut your sorry ass tongue out." Mack pulled his knife and continued, "C'mon, say just one more word. I don't care if it's just a scream of pain, say something, dammit!"

Halfway through a half-hearted 'piss on you', Wills Boren lost his teeth, to a boot heel. Through bloody lips, Mack jerked the man's tongue as far as it would pull, and sliced it off with his razor-sharp blade.

"We're not going to bother the lawmen with this little incident," Mack said as he removed Bob's rope from the fallen man. He threw it over a low hanging pine limb, then placed it around the crying man's neck, dragging him to his feet.

Webfoot grabbed the man's arms, tied his elbows behind him, and told Mack, "I wanna be th' one t' string this bastard up, Mack. I ain't got no fam'ly no where 'round here. Bob, he got kids all o'er th' place, even iffen he don't claim 'em.

"You still young 'n you gonna have a fam'ly someday. Me, I jist don' give a damn, an' I ain't got no body t' look down at me."

Mack handed Webfoot the other end of the rope. With three wraps, and a cinch around the saddle horn, Webfoot walked his horse forward until Wills' head hit the bottom of the limb.

"This here's whut that God damn Blackie d'zerved." Bob said, "Brody killed his ass too quick. He shoulda suffer'd first. His ol' daddy was jist as sorry. He beat his poor wife, 'n sold her body t' any ol' drifter comin' thru town. She got ahold of a ten guage 'n blowed his haid off. Broke her arm shootin' thet cannon, but ol' Judd never even took a step. *He* shoulda suffered, too. She ran Blackie off, 'n finally lef' town 'n went east, somewheres."

The fight, Millie had put up, was enough delay to keep her abductors from violating her before Mack, Brody and the others arrived. She held onto Brody with all her strength.

Brody mounted his horse, lifted Millie into his lap, and rode past the hanging Wills Boren without even looking up.

Mack and the others loaded the dead men into their own wagon, and returned to town, where the bodies were turned over to the undertaker.

The town marshal saw who the dead men were, turned to the three Longhorn drivers and said, "Curt was wondering where you three went to, said you got lumber to haul." With that said, he turned and walked away.

The ten day trip to Kansas City was just what Mack needed to settle himself down, and think more about his future with Lucy. He and Bob made good time, and had very little problem finding the right facilities and people to handle Longhorn's needs along the Kansas City route.

Curt had arranged for six tons of feed corn and oats to be loaded onto the tandems for the return trip. Three and one-half tons were on Bob's rig, two and one-half on Mack's. Mack could travel faster, with the lighter load, so the detour to pick up his mother was no problem. They caught up with Bob at the last way station, then traveled together the rest of the way.

"Mack," Bob said to the young man, "I didn' thank you'd e'er tell me a lie, boy, but I kin see right now, yer in a heap o' trouble soon's we gits back ta home. Ya tol' me you'ze goin' after yer maw. Miss Lucy's gonna be mighty upset when ya shows up with *thet* pretty gal sittin' b'side ya." He tipped his ragged, old hat to Mack's mother. "Cain't no way thet li'l lady could be ol' 'nuff t' have a big, ugly pup yer age."

"Drive your wagon, Bob," Mack called to him, as he was climbing onto the wagon seat, "And don't you be makin' eyes at my mother. I'd hate to ruin my good reputation by givin' an old man a good ass-whippin'."

"Yeah?" Bob countered, "It might be *yore* th' one thet'll have ta 'splain how an ol' man whupped yer *own* ass." Bob smiled at the woman, winked at her, then slapped the reins on the team's backs. "Hyaw! Git up thar, Flossie! Hyaw! Lets go, we gotta git home!"

Lucy and Christina MacKenzie became immediate friends. "You don't need to be calling me 'Mrs.' or any other names, either, Lucy dear, just call me 'mom', 'maw', or whatever you're comfortable with. Lots of people call me 'Chris'. From what Mack tells me, we'll be related soon, anyway. Might as well start getting used to it."

"What does Mack usually call you?" Lucy asked, "I'll just call you the same."

"Christina smiled at her future daughter-in-law and said, "Mack has never called me anything, but 'mother'. He's always been big, like his paw. He's always had the toughness of my father. But, he's the sweetest son any woman could ever have."

"I'll tell you a story, Lucy dear. It was a horrible thing that happened about five years ago. Mack will probably never talk about it, but if you're going to be his wife, you need to know.

"My husband was plowing a new wheat field. He and his team were near a stand of cottonwoods, which were close to Black Bull Creek, about half a mile from our house. A pack of dogs attacked him, and his mules. One of the mules went down, the other one broke loose and headed for home. Roscoe was bitten several times, but after the mule fell, the dogs concentrated on killing it, and Roscoe was able to get away.

Tears were welling up in Christina's eyes as she continued, "Two days later, Roscoe, Beatrice and Gloria, our daughters, were in the barn. The girls decided to pull a prank on their paw. Roscoe was bending over a feed box when Gloria slipped a soft, wet, rope into the edge of his pants leg." The tears were now ambling, slowly down her cheeks. "Beatrice hollered *SNAKE!* Roscoe grabbed both of my girls and started beating them."

Christina hesitated, drew a couple of deep breaths, composed herself, and went on, "Their paw never laid a finger on those girls in their lives, before that day. He went crazy, beating, kicking them and even biting their faces and arms. Mack heard the screaming, ran to the barn, and hit his paw with a grubbing hoe.

"Roscoe turned on him, but Mack hit him again. He went down, Mack tied him to a post, and helped his sisters to the house. Then he rode to town, and brought the doctor back. Roscoe never came to, again. Mack feels like he killed his father, but the doctor said it was the rabies. Over the next six days, Mack and I had to watch his sisters die a terribly painful death, tied to their beds, so they wouldn't hurt anybody."

Lucy's tears were flowing as much as Christina's as the story went on, "Mack became a full grown, responsible man, at the age of sixteen. He dug graves, buried Roscoe and his big sisters, then took care of me, which was the hardest job of all.

"I wasn't able to look at the girls' room anymore. I couldn't sleep. I couldn't eat. I just didn't even care if I even lived, anymore. So much had been taken from me. Then one day, Mack put his big, strong, leathery hands on each side of my face. I realized that the love in those hands made it the softest touch I'd ever felt.

"He told me he'd take care of me, he'd never leave home, and he loved me. He said we'd find another farm and get rid of the one with the bad memories. He told me that he and God would look after me for the rest of my days."

Christina relaxed her shoulders, took more deep breaths, and said, "That was two months after they died. I realized, finally, Mack had been telling me the same things every day. It just took me that long, to wake up and hear him.

"I found out that he, and his friend, Ricky, located the dog pack, and shot the ones that were still alive.

"Over the last few years, we sold the farm, but still lived there. The man who bought it had a nice home, and let us keep living there, rent free. Mack worked the same fields he had worked with his daddy, and trained horses and mules, for everybody around. He's a great trainer, too, Lucy, he can do it all. From plow mules to race horses, he can train them. Oh, just listen to me brag! You'll see soon enough.

"Anyway, a while back, the man who bought our farm told us that his daughter was getting married, next summer. He wanted to let her and her husband have our place as a wedding gift. He never told us we had to move, but it was time we left there. That's when Mack came out this way looking for work."

Lucy took Christina into her arms and held her tightly, rocking gently until both women had run out of tears. "Thank you, Mother," she said, finally, "I'll never ask Mack a thing about his father or sisters. If he decides to tell me anything, I'll know what to expect. "I'm so happy you're here with us, now. Sometimes, it seems like the only people I have around to talk to are men, and you *know* how frustrating *that* can be."

The women shared a light laugh, which sealed the bond between them.

EPILOGUE

Brody Hornsby married Millie White. He had no interest in the shipping business, but became a partner with Peterman Logging.

After Brody transferred to Wyoming, Curt sold his portion of Longhorn Express to Whiskers Long, so he could move to Wyoming, also, to be near his two grandsons.

After twenty years of driving freight wagons, Whiskers and his second wife, Cassie, the former madam of the brothel in Perro Loco, turned the business over to their only heirs, Lucy and Mack.

'Daddy' and 'Maw', as Lucy called them, moved to Albuquerque, New Mexico. There, they set up a lucrative business selling the horses that Mack and his son trained.

Bob courted Christina MacKenzie throughout the winter months. He finally gave in to his feelings and they were married in the following April.

Lucy MacKenzie gave birth to four children, one son and three daughters, all four of whom could ride, rope, and make damn good coffee, before the age of six.

That's What Friends Are For

"Just a couple more hours and you'll be home, Red." Jack Casey was talking to his best friend, Red Wolf Patterson. Red Wolf was an eighteen year old, full blood, Lakota Sioux. Patterson was the surname given to him at the white man's school, in Pittsburg.

Jack's father was an instructor at the same school, so consequently, Jack,went to the same classes as Red Wolf, for the last four years. The school was established to educate the 'red heathens' in the ways of the white man, then return them to their people, hoping that they would, in turn, educate more Indians. The stated intent was that, if the Indians understood the white men better, the process of living in co-inhabited areas would be safer and more beneficial to all. In truth, the white men wanted all they could get, and wanted the Indians to move back and accept it.

Jack was two years older than Red Wolf, and had spent five years in a private military school, where he excelled in marksmanship, as well as academically. When he learned that his father was going to be teaching Indian children, he requested to attend the same school. Jack was a bright young man and wanted to learn as much as he could about these Native Americans. As a result of Red Wolf's friendship, he had learned much of the Sioux language and sign language, which was much the same in all the Indian nations.

Because of the importance of the school's mission, the school administrator sent weekly reports to the Bureau of Indian Affairs (B.I.A.) on the progress of those children being educated there. The B.I.A. kept a close eye on the reports of Red Wolf's exceptional progress, and that of his friend, Jack Casey. Because of his achievements at the military school, the B.I.A already had an extensive file, on Jack, from that institution.

Unknown to most people, even his father, Jack had been summoned, one weekend, to Washington, by the War Department, and was issued a commission as a Captain in the United States Army. He was also issued a letter of introduction, along with instructions to all military personnel, 'to provide complete cooperation and assistance upon Jack's request'. His mission; "to observe and report the progress of acclimating the Sioux into a productive society." Exactly what those words meant was still a question in Jack Casey's mind.

His friend, Red Wolf Patterson, was not a hostile savage. Nor was any of the other young Indians being taught at the school. As far as Jack could tell, the pranks and jokes were no worse than those done by white youngsters. The Indians were quick learners, and most were very intelligent.

"That's right, Jackie boy", said Red Wolf "just a couple of more hours and you can meet my mother, father, and my two sisters. You better be a nice white man, too, or they will make a steer out of you, fatten you up, and feed you to the chiefs at the next big gathering. But, if you're a nice man, I might let you sleep just outside my lodge, with my dogs, if they like you".

The trip from Pittsburg had been uneventful, for the most part. The worst part was the train ride. No matter what part of the train you were in, the smoke seeped into your car, making eyes sting and water. It took two washings, at the Chinese laundry in Kansas City, to get the smell out of their clothes.

The consolation, for having to spend two nights in town, was the ladies. Betty and Marie were very nice looking prostitutes, were fun, and not overly expensive. The men were sitting in The Palace, which was the finest restaurant in town. The girls were absent for a few minutes, attending to their 'needs' at the oversized privy, behind the building. Red Wolf teased Jack about staying in Kansas City and raising a family. "Jack and Betty, sittin' in a tree, K-I-S-S-I-N-G, first comes lov . . . ."

"Be careful, Red, it's been a long time since I kicked your ugly ass" Jack quipped, grinning. "I'd hate to have to embarrass you here, in this fine establishment".

"Little brother, you've never, *ever*, kicked my ass. In fact, you've never even been able to get close enough to give me a bloody nose," which was the truth. Jack was fast, strong, and could hold his own in any situation, whether it was a fight or a debate.

Except with Red Wolf. His strength and agility were staggering. No matter what kind of fisticuffs his opponent wished to engage in, nobody could match Red Wolf Patterson.

"You'll have to agree with me, though, Red," Jack said, "Betty and Marie are girls who deserve more than they have. They really should have homes, husbands and kids. They shouldn't have to sell themselves to make a living. Hey! I just thought of something. Do you remember Miss Harrison? The one who used to teach us mathematics? She has a big dress shop in St. Louis, now. She ships dresses everywhere. I'm going to wire her, and see if she can use some help". Jack was up and out the door in seconds.

When the girls returned, Red Wolf told them that Jack would be right back, he had gone to send a wire. About 45 minutes later, Jack returned and gave the "all is well" sign to his friend. They had a discussion with the girls. As it turned out, both were adept at sewing, and were willing to give up their current "trade", ... after one more night with these guys.

Jack bought one-way tickets, for both girls, to St. Louis on the afternoon train. When it pulled out, he and Red Wolf mounted up and headed north.

Now, they were in Sioux lands, and getting very close to the village where Red Wolf grew up. "The truth is, little brother, I was afraid Betty was gonna trap you and keep you in the city. Then, I wouldn't be able to set you up with my big sister, Snow Rabbit. She's your age, very old, and needs a man to provide for her. You'll like her, she can skin and butcher a buffalo faster than any woman in our village. Looks good, too, for a sister. You could be my brother-in-law. Don't thank me, that's what friends are for".

Jack smiled and said, casually, "If she looks like you, no thanks."

Red Wolf spotted a small wisp of smoke. "Look, little brother, there it is. Let's go!" They put the horses into a full run and in a few minutes, they crossed the shallow stream and rode into camp.

Red Wolf's family, as well as the rest of the village, turned out to give the travelers a hearty welcome. Jack saw a lovely, young woman smiling at him, and hoped it was Red Wolf's sister. A soft voice called from behind him, in the Sioux language, "Welcome home, little brother". Jack and Red Wolf turned, at the same time, to see a beautiful, very pregnant, woman.

Red Wolf grabbed her, hugged her, and yelled, "Whoa! What's all this?" he asked as he rubbed her belly.

"Bad Arm and I were married, nearly a year ago, little brother. Didn't you get the letter the white man took to you?"

"No, I didn't get a letter. Where is Bad Arm? He's a good man. When will the baby get here? Is Mother and Father alright? Where is Little Bird?'

"Slow down, Red Wolf, everyone is fine and the baby will be here next month, if his uncle doesn't get him so excited that he wants to get out of here sooner." she replied.

"Mother and Father are right behind you, beside their new lodge. Little Bird is right over there, close to Bad Arm, smiling much too big, at your friend."

"What? That's Little Bird? I can't believe she's that grown up. She's not smiling at Jack. She can't be smiling at Jack. Oh, hell, she is smiling at Jack."

After all the introductions were made, Jack was given a tour of the village by Snow Rabbit and Bad Arm. He was pleasing surprised at the organization and cleanliness of the camp. Many cities could take lessons from those considered as 'heathens'. Snow, as her family called her, spoke enough English to converse with Jack, but was pleased when he asked if they could use Sioux, because he needed the practice. Jack also decided that Bad Arm was a lucky man, to have the love of this smart, attractive woman.

Returning to the lodge, Jack was met by Red Wolf. "There is a problem, Jack." Red Wolf only call Jack by his name when something was serious was in the air. "My sister is interested in you, and that's not good."

"But she and Bad Arm seem to be very happy together." Jack countered.

"No, not Snow, ... It's Little Bird. She told Mother that she wanted to know you much better, and maybe make you her husband! She's only sixteen! Of course, that *is* the age most Sioux women marry. It took Snow much longer to make up her mind. But it's my little sister, Jack, so don't do anything to hurt her. Or else I'll make a steer out of you, myself." As Red wolf walked away, Jack was left standing in the middle of camp, totally deflated, and wondering if he had made a mistake coming to South Dakota.

Two days later, the morning dawned with some heavy clouds in the east. Little Bird had taken it upon herself to see to it, that Jack was fed good, under the scrutinizing eyes of Red Wolf. "Looks like we could get some rain, later, little brother." Red Wolf had concern in his voice. "If it looks like it will be too heavy, the camp will move up the hill, to higher ground. Most of the year, it's dry enough to stay put, but once in a while, the stream becomes a river. It only takes two or three hours to move camp, and we can usually move back a couple days later."

"I'm just a guest here, Red, but tell me if there is anything I can do to help."

"Just be ready to help, if we need to move. The women move most of the village, and the men see to it that the stock and old people get to safety."

As the young men sat and talked, they heard a rumble of thunder, in the distance. After listening to the rumble for several seconds, without interruption, Red Wolf jumped up and yelled "Flood!!! Everyone run!!" As Jack jumped up, Red Wolf called to him to cut the horses loose, and get up the hill.

Just as Jack jerked the knot on the rope corral. He heard screaming, over the roar of the wall of water, which was nearly upon them. The horses' instinct took them uphill, but Jack could see that he would never make it. He caught a low hanging limb, swung up into the fork of a large tree, and climbed higher, as his boots were getting wet from the rising water.

He managed to climb high enough to avoid being swept away, but as he looked around, he could see that others had been caught unaware, and were trying to swim, against the strong current, to the bank.

Jack knew that the crash of the frontal wall, of water, was the most dangerous part of a flash flood. He was an accomplished swimmer, and knew he was capable of helping some of those who were in the water. He quickly removed his boots, wedged then into a tree fork, stuck his wallet inside one of them and dived toward a small boy. He managed to get the boy to hold onto his neck, and swam to bank of the creek, turned river. A woman, maybe the boy's mother, was waiting and took him from Jack. Jack immediately dived in again, and went toward another child. He grabbed the boy by the shirt, and pulled him to bank, where the same woman took him.

A body was floating along, but Jack saw an arm move. He was in the water again. This time an old woman was rescued. The woman on the bank had been replaced by two others. Jack then saw other men diving in, or already swimming to others. 'Reinforcements' was the only word that came to his mind. In he went again. As he reached a struggling woman, he pulled her around to face him. It was Snow Rabbit. Ordinarily a good swimmer, she was handicapped now, with an extra twenty pounds in her stomach. She put her arms around his neck, with her stomach against his back. He was tiring, but there was no way he was going to let this one die.

Little Bird was at the shoreline when Jack pulled his sore, tired body up with Snow holding on. She helped her sister up the hill, as Jack looked back at the river. It had already started to recede, but there were still people who needed help. He rescued four more, including an old man and three little girls. It still had not rained in the village, itself.

The Sioux women were amazing. Fires were built immediately. Clothes were drying on racks which were assembled in minutes. Children were being herded together and inventoried. Families were assigned to specific areas, in order for other family members to locate them.

The men set about rounding up horses, and the steers the B.I.A. had sent to them, the previous week. After retrieving his boots and wallet, Jack started helping the old and injured to find their families. Each reunion brought a tear to his eye, as he witnessed the joy of a family welcoming their elders, or their children.

Red Wolf rode in and told Jack that the round-up was successful, for the most part, but the biggest loss was the lodges, food, bedding, cooking utensils, clothing and other things usually found within the lodges. Red Wolf dismounted, grasped forearms with Jack, then hugged him to his chest. "Thank you, little brother", he spoke softly, "It looks like we lost two children, one old man, and one old woman. It would have been much worse if you hadn't been here to help. You saved Snow Rabbit. No man has ever had a better sister." He looked deep into Jack's tear filled eyes. "No man has ever had a better brother."

"Like you told me, when we left St. Louis," Jack said, "No need to thank me, that's what friends are for.

"Now, Red, I need to use two good horses. I'll be gone three or four days, but I'm going to get some help, if I can. Meantime, food is the most important thing".

"Yes, little brother, we already have men traveling downstream to see what they can find. We also have hunters leaving, in a few minutes. It'll be hard, but we'll be alright."

Jack rode hard, switching mounts as needed. Twenty hours later, he rode into Fort Robinson, Nebraska. When the guard on duty tried to question him, the weariness brought out the agitated and assertive side of him, that few people had ever seen. "Stand at attention when you talk to me, soldier! I'm U.S. Army Captain, Jack Casey! Now get me your officer on duty, now!" Jack quickly showed his identification, and insisted on a meeting with the fort's commanding officer.

"I need four wagons, fill them with food, canvas, pots and pans, material for clothes, and . . . . I want fifty rifles, repeaters, along with two hundred rounds of ammunition for each one. I want the wagons loaded and ready to go in two hours." "Now wait a minute, Captain Casey," Colonel Jones started, but Jack cut him off, "Colonel, you read the instructions in my letter, either you do as I request, or I'll wire Washington. You could be relieved of your commission in as little as 45 minutes. I suggest you start giving orders."

Two days later, Jack left the wagons on horseback. He had been able to get some badly needed rest in the back of one of them, by sleeping on a stack of canvas. He left directions with the sergeant in charge, and an order to keep the wagons moving as much as possible. The sergeant liked Jack, and told him that, as long it wouldn't harm the mules, the wagon would be moving. Jack took three of the new rifles, and six boxes of shells with him, as well as his own weapons. Five hours after leaving the wagons, he rode into the Sioux village. It would take the wagons until late the next day to arrive.

Little Bird was one of the first to see Jack when he rode in. Her shrill yell alerted the rest of the camp and most of the people came running to greet him. Red Wolf had just returned from a hunting trip, but one with limited success. As Jack and his Sioux brother were about to greet each other, Little Bird threw her arms around Jack and was babbling so fast that Jack missed most of what she was saying. She said something about "pretty man" and "the water", "Snow Rabbit", "boy child" and "more children". Red Wolf placed his strong hands on his little sister's shoulders, and gently moved her back. She remained standing, her eyes on Jack, and smiling. Tears were in her eyes.

"What was all that about, Red?" Jack asked.

Red Wolf chuckled, "Well, first of all, she was going on about you, the pretty man, ... She can't see very well . . . . Then she was thanking you for pulling our people out of the water. Especially Snow Rabbit. All the excitement sent Snow into birthing pains. There is a new member in our family. He is named already. Snow named him for his father, mother and his new uncle. His name is Bad Jack Rabbit. He screams a war whoop louder that a coyote can howl. Oh yes . . . . Little Bird also said that you and her would make more children, for the People. Be careful, little brother, she *is* my little sister," he said with a smile.

Jack handed one of the new rifles to Red Wolf. "These are for you, Bad Arm, and Wolf Tooth." Wolf Tooth was Red Wolf's father. "Four wagons will be here tomorrow, with supplies for your village. There will be 47 more rifles like these. You, your father, and Bad Arm will decide who will get them. Pick men who can see well, men who can think fast, and those loyal to the People. The soldiers, with the wagons, will train your men how to use these new style rifles. These rifles can shoot nine times, without reloading. Even you, Red, should be able to get close enough, to get a buffalo, occasionally." As Red Wolf opened his mouth to speak, Jack held up his hand, "No need to thank me, that's what friends are for. Now, I'm hungry. You got anything to eat?"

When Jack woke up the next morning, Little Bird was asleep, beside him. He jumped up, startling her. When she squealed, Red Wolf, and his parents came up like it was a signal of danger. Jack started to explain that he knew nothing about why Little Bird was sleeping beside him. Red Wolf stopped him and told him that she considered herself to be Jack's wife. The gift of the rifles, the saving of Snow, and the supplies, in route, were worth more than four good horses, the usual payment for a Sioux bride. "She has her mind made up, little brother, Hey! Now you really are my brother".

"Now wait a minute, Red, I think I have a say in this thing, and I'm not ready to be married," Jack protested. "Little Bird is a fine, young woman, and there are many warriors here that would be proud to marry a beautiful girl, like her. I think she just likes the idea of a handsome, white, hero for a husband." He grinned.

Red wolf's mother spoke up and told Jack that Little Rabbit's mind was made up the day they first rode into camp. "You are handsome and a hero, but every person in the village already considers you as their brother. You have white blood in your body, but you are one of the People. Little Bird is your wife. I have spoken." As if to emphasize her status as matriarch, she laid her hand on the handle of the newly knapped, flint knife in her belt.

Red Wolf told Jack that Little Bird would honor any request of her new husband. She would cook, sew, build lodges, warm his bed, raise his children, skin and butcher his game. "You'll love her, little brother, she's a wonderful girl. She'll be a much better wife than Betty would have." Jack threw a soft punch at his friend. Red Wolf leaned close and whispered, "No need to thank me, that's what friends are for."

Against useless and feeble protests, from Jack, a new lodge was built from the canvas, brought from Fort Robinson. He and Little Bird were moved in and, during the third night, Jack finally gave in, and they made love, consummating their union . . . . Then three more times . . . . It was the happiest night he had ever spent with a woman, and he admitted, to himself, that he was falling in love . . . . with his wife.

EPILOGUE

Jack Casey lived with the Sioux for twelve years. He was active in assuring that the People were treated fairly, and he dealt with encroaching settlers on a continuing basis. He and Little Bird, eventually, moved to a ranch in northern Nebraska, where they raised their three daughters.

Red Wolf Patterson didn't marry until he was nearly thirty, although it was rumored that he had fathered several youngsters, in South Dakota and northern Nebraska.

He was appointed U.S. Marshal, and served in that capacity for over twenty years, and was widely known for his honesty and fairness. His custom Colt Peacemaker rested on his left hip, in a hand-tooled holster. Engraved on it were the words, "That's what friends are for."

Max and Maggie

Max watched the buzzards circling, . . . and circling, . . . and circling. They were getting lower, again. He had never seen so many, at one time. He was out of shells, now. Every time he had shot one, the rest had flown away, but not far. Now, his gun and gun belt were both empty. Dead buzzards were littering the ground around him. The shots hadn't fazed the ones who were feasting on the horse. It was lying, perhaps, a quarter mile away. Max had managed to drag himself this far, even with the broken arm and leg.

It had been about this same time yesterday, he thought it was just yesterday, when his horse stepped in a hole. 'Probably a gopher hole' he said aloud, 'they get pretty big in this part of West Texas.' Even with his pain, Max had enough presence of mind to know the horse was hurt, bad hurt. He couldn't muster enough strength to pull his Winchester from the saddle scabbard. The horse was lying on it. He had raised his single action Colt, left handed, cock it and squeezed the trigger. The pistol had bucked hard, but the horse was no longer in pain . . . .

"Hell, boy!", the old man's voice was loud. "It's 'bout time you woke your lazy ass up! You been layin' there more'n four days. Anybody young as you shouldn't be letting' a cupple o' broken limbs keep you down more'n 'bout a day, mebbe day 'n a half."

Max had opened his eyes a few minutes before. A woman was in the room, at a wash basin. She stepped out, as soon as she saw Max was awake. The old timer had come in, right away, and started in.

"'Sides that, you been bleedin' all over them sheets, 'n Maggie's been tryin' to keep up with cleanin' *and* doctorin' you. 'Ats been purty tough on her, too, bein' in a family way, like she is."

The woman re-entered the room with a bundle of sheets and towels. "That's enough, Paw, leave the man alone. He's in pain and he doesn't need

116

you fussing at him. Fetch him some water, and if that sets ok, we'll try him on some beans, in a little while. Tell Deke he's awake, he'll want to talk to the gentleman, if he's strong enough."

As the old man was leaving, Max heard him grumbling something about 'ungrateful kids, . . . always bitchin', . . . not too big to still get their ass whupped.' Max couldn't help but laugh a little. Paw returned within a matter of seconds with a pitcher of water and a cup. As he poured, he told Max, "Yore a lucky boy. Deke hadn't found you when he did, you'da been jist a pile of bones, now. He said them buzzerds was settin' the table and askin' the Lord to bless their meal, when him and ol' Dobie rode up on you. Said if you could shoot men as good as you do buzzards, you'd be a bad one to deal with."

Max wanted to gulp the water down, but knew better. Doing that would only result in its coming right back up. He sipped, slowly, and emptied the cup in four or five minutes. The old man refilled it, and Max took another sip. "Are you *sure* I'm not dead? You could be the devil. As bad as I hurt, this could be hell." He grinned and his lip split.

"Ouch! Now see what you've done, old timer. You wounded me."

The woman snickered, but the old man started in, again. "Wounded you, my ass, if I'd a'done it, it woulda killed you. Hand this pup a rag, Maggie, his 'poor widdle wip is bweedin'. Who are you, boy, and what you doin' in these parts?"

Max pressed the wet rag to his lip, looked at it, pressed it again and spoke, "I'm Max Sanders. I was on my way to Lubbock. I was thrown from my horse when it stepped in a hole. His leg broke and I had to kill him. The last thing I remember was buzzards circling, and I was hurting, ... Bad." Max's voice was coarse. His throat was still dry. He sipped some more water. "Where am I?"

"Paw, please go on and tell Deke our guest is awake." The woman's voice was beautiful. The old man left, mumbling. She spoke up, "Hi, I'm Maggie Reddy. My husband, Deke Reddy, was on his way to town, a few days ago. He heard a shot, it must have been your last one, and he noticed the big flock of buzzards. When he found you, two of them were tearing at your wounded arm. You're going to have a bad scar. It was closer to bring you here, than to take you on into town. You've been unconscious for four days. Actually, that's probably a good thing, because the doc came out, set your broken leg and arm, and patched you up. Like paw said, I've been dressing your wounds since. Do you think you're ready to try some beans? This pot full turned out real good."

Sam told her he was ready, and she left, just as a tall, slim man, wearing an over-sized hat came in. "Howdy. I'm Deke Reddy. Welcome to hell," he chuckled. "Paw told me what you said. You got one part right, for sure. That old man's the devil." Deke extended his left hand, knowing Max couldn't shake with his right. He then explained that, after he'd brought Max to the ranch house, he'd returned to the dead horse, to retrieve his saddle, rifle, and other possessions. All were stored in the tack room, inside the barn. Max thanked him. Nearly everything he owned was on that horse, and on his back. Now, the clothes he had been wearing were ruined. His other set of clothes were in his saddlebags.

"I have money in my pack, that was on my horse. I'll gladly pay y'all for all the trouble." Max said. "I'll buy another horse, if you'd be kind enough to find me one, and as soon as I can ride, I'll get out of y'all's hair."

Deke told him not to worry too much, they had plenty of room and Maggie now had something else to help occupy her mind. She had already made all the blankets the new baby would need, crocheted booties, caps, and who knows what else. There was little to do, between sunup, and sundown. That was when the men left for the day, and when they returned.

Sophia, the Mexican housekeeper, was doing most of the cleaning and cooking, now, but Maggie had to oversee the seasoning. "Sophia tends to go a little overboard on the hot stuff. Maggie and Fred, Maggie's brother, can't quite handle her red chili peppers, which she puts in everything. The rest of us can add what we want, after it's on our plates."

"Now don't start in on Sophia, Deke," Maggie was returning with the beans, "She is a fine cook, and I don't know what I'd do without her. Y'all can talk later, Mr. Sanders needs to try to eat."

Max told Maggie "No, no, please, it's just Max." Maggie smiled and said "Fine. Max it is. You can call all of us by our first names, too."

After sampling a few mashed up beans, Max told her that her beans were 'better 'n snuff', the best I've ever had.' Whether they were or not, it made Maggie feel good because she had cooked this batch, herself.

Two days later, Max was strong enough to sit in the front room. Fred and Deke had helped him to a rocker, and elevated his broken, left leg. Paw was giving instructions, through the whole procedure. "Git them pillers off my bed, Fred, they's thicker and his laig will be easier on it. If'n you pull that table over close, Maggie, he can rest that bad arm on it. No, wait a damn minute, girl, y'ain't needin' to be movin' stuff. I'll git it myself."

The four of them couldn't believe Paw was fussing over Max, like a wet hen over her chicks.

Over the last two days, Max and Maggie had spent several hours talking. Paw was actually her, and Fred's, grandfather. He had settled on this land more than fifty years ago, with their grandmother. Over the decades, he had dealt with Indians, rustlers, drought, and the loss of his wife and two children, one being Maggie's mother. Maggie and Fred would inherit the place, nearly three thousand acres, when he finally decided to leave Texas, bound for hell. He was always telling people, "I'll never see Margaret again. (Maggie was named after her grandmother) She got wings, I'll get a pitchfork." He had given instructions for Fred and Deke to 'build his box outta bo-dark' (bois d'arc) because 'when I hit's the fires o'hell, it'll be poppin' so much, all my ol' friends will know I got there.' It had been 14 years since Margaret had passed away.

The last ten years, or so, had been pretty uneventful, except for finding Max. the ranch held 900 head of cattle, about 300 horses, and a few goats. The goats were kept close to the house. They ate weeds, briars, etc. first, and grass last. By keeping the vegetation cropped short, snakes were rarely a problem around their home.

Max decided these people were genuinely, honest, hard-working people, so he told Maggie about himself, about a week later.

He had been raised west of San Antonio, near an old settlement named Castroville. The first settlers were German immigrants, and Max's mother was a descendant of one of the founders.

Max was raised to respect all people, at least until someone proved themselves not worthy of respect. He learned to work hard, ride, rope and shoot very early in his life. His chest and arms were like his father's, very strong. His legs, stout, but not near as long as Deke's. He had been a wrangler, drover, and hunter, all before he turned twenty. In 1881, Max took a job in San Antonio as a deputy sheriff of Bexar County. Four years later, as a result of his good work and reputation for being firm, yet fair, he was contacted about becoming the City Marshal of Lubbock.

His parents had died in a fire when he was fourteen, and his older sister had taken him in. She, and her husband, now had teenagers of their own.

Since there was no particular obligations to keep him in San Antonio, he had packed his roll onto his horse and headed toward Lubbock.

"And that's why you're in the Abilene area" Maggie concluded.

"Yep, I guess when I get strong enough, I'll go into town and send a wire to the town council, out there, and see if they've filled the job, yet."

"The doctor said it'll be at least four more weeks before you can ride, then you'll have to go easy on that leg. The break wasn't as clean as the one in your arm, and it'll take longer, for it to heal right." Maggie could tell that Max was getting 'house bound'. "Fred made you some crutches from an old bedstead, and the doctor says you can start moving around more next week, if you feel like it."

"Well, it will be nice to go to the outhouse when I need to, so you won't have to empty my slop jar for me. Fred and Deke won't have to help me get dressed, if you can call wearing my drawers, and this house coat 'being dressed'."

Maggie chuckled and said, "It's not much problem. If you're still here when the baby's born, you may have to empty my slop jar." They both laughed and were talking about baby names when Paw came in.

"Whut in thunderation are you two cackling about? Ain't they some work y'all could be doin'?" He pointed at Maggie, "Not too much fer you, though, girly. My great-grandson ain't ready for no hard work, yet. And you, Maxie boy, you need to figger out somethin' you can do to hep out 'round here. It's costin' a bundle to feed yore lazy butt. Jist you don't do anything thet'll make things worse. The sooner you git well, the quicker we'll git rid of ya."

"Someone put a burr in your britches this morning?" Max asked. "You're usual bright, smiling personality just doesn't seem to be there."

Maggie smiled at him as he prodded Paw.

"Don't you start with me" Paw said, "Deke and Fred already ran off and left all the work 'round here fer me do. An' me with my rhumatiz like it is." Max looked at the old man. '*If I live to be as old as him,*' he thought, '*I hope my rheumatism keeps me going all day long, like it does for him.*' The man was somewhere in his sixties, but was the first one up in the morning. As soon as he drank three or four cups of coffee, he was out the door. His time was spent, mostly, around the house, barn, and corral. The majority of the livestock and field work were done by Deke, Fred and two hired hands, although Paw was still very capable of riding, roping, branding and building fence.

"Soon's you can git up an' 'round, you kin help me clean the stalls in the barn." Paw fussed, "Thet'll be good exercise fer ya. 'Less you cain't stand to git the smell of horse shit on yer boots, then you kin jist set on yer butt an' git fat".

"Now don't go blaming the horses for that smell you bring in here with you," Max countered, "I've been here a little over two weeks and you ain't taken a bath in all that time. In fact, I've been told the horses turn up their noses when you walk into the barn. I've got a broken leg and arm, but I've had three baths in the same two weeks."

"Yeah, well. Yer wastin' water." the old man answered. "When y'ain't doin' nuthin', y'ain't gittin dirty."

As Paw went back out the door, Max and Maggie burst into laughter. "I love the way you hold your own with him." Maggie said. "Fred's never been able to fuss back at Paw. Deke just smiles, ignores him and goes on about his business. I think it's good for the old stinker." She giggled and added, "I did say *STINKER*, didn't I?" They both laughed again.

Max enjoyed Maggie's laugh. He enjoyed her movements, her smiles, that beautiful voice when she was humming, or singing, softly, like she did often. Max had never felt as close to any woman. "*I'm going to miss her a lot, when I leave.*" he thought. "*Too much. Why couldn't I have met her in San Antonio? She's married and expecting a baby, Deke's baby, before long. What a wonderful woman she is.*

"*Stop it Max!*" he thought to himself. "*Dammit, she's happy here with her family, and I just need to get well enough to get the hell out of here. Get out of her way, and get her out of my mind. No, that'll never happen, I'll always remember Maggie.*"

"What are you thinking about so seriously?" Maggie broke his train of thought.

"Uh, just thinking of the past, and what's going to happen tomorrow, or the next day, or the next." He replied. "Nobody knows what the future holds for them. You just gotta plan for something, and hope it works out. I was planning to be in Lubbock by now, and look where I am. Six miles south of Abilene, with a broken arm, a broken leg, putting up with a gripey old man, and enjoying the company of the most wonderful woman I've ever known." '*No! Did I just say that? Damn! . . . . Damn! Why did I say that?*' Max thought. '*I've messed up now, ... Damn!*'

He looked up at Maggie. She was smiling. There was a small tear in her eye. "Thank you, Max. That's the nicest thing anyone has ever said about me." She walked over to him, put one arm around his neck, the other hand around his head, and hugged him to her swollen belly. "You're a fine man, Max Sanders. One day you'll make some lucky woman a fine husband, too." She patted his head, and walked into the other room.

"I love you, Maggie. I'll always wish you were that woman." He thought.

Max started using his crutches during the next week. He began hobbling to the barn and corral area, mostly to give Paw a hard time about one thing or another.

"Dammit, boy, cain't you git back in the house 'n warsh dishes fer Maggie, or sumthin?" Paw asked him one morning.

Max laughed and replied, "Are you kiddin '? She just got through running me out. Said I was under foot. I think her and Sophia was up to something and I was in the way."

"Well boy, whut do ya think you can do t' help out here?" Paw asked. Ya cain't handle a shovel or a pitchfork, with thet game arm. Mebbe you kin jist point yer finger, 'n show this igner'nt old man something I need t' do."

Max asked where the tack room was, then went inside the barn to find it. Once inside, he found his own gear. Nothing had been untied, unbuckled, nor messed with in any manner, as far as he could tell. His rifle, saddle and bridle had been thoroughly cleaned, though. He lifted his saddle bags from the rail and pulled a roll of cash from the left one, it was all there. Putting them back on the rail presented a harder challenge, using his left arm, only. He noticed that some of the other gear in the room was in need of repair.

When he found large board, he managed to wrestle it into place between stall slats, which made a suitable table. Finding an empty nail keg to sit on, Max hobbled in and out, bringing stirrups, bridles, and pieces of harness to the pile he was making, near the table. He called out to Paw and asked if there were any brads or rivets in the barn.

"You hollerin' at me, boy?" Paw asked.

Max told him, "No, I was *hollerin'* at that other old goat." He pointed at shaggy ram in the yard. "He's the one with the nice disposition."

"Don't be a smart ass, whut you want?"

Max told him that with some brads, rivets, a good leather punch and a small hammer, he could fix most of the tack he'd gathered up. He had figured a way to rest his right arm on the table, and use it to hold things still. He could do most of the other work with his left hand. He had learned to rope, and shoot left handed, when he was younger, and was nearly as good at that as he was right handed. Paw got the tools, and within minutes, Max was at work.

About an hour, or so, later, a loud scream came from inside the house. As Max was grabbing his crutches, he saw Paw sail over the corral fence and hit the ground running. By the time Max reached the house, he heard a baby crying. Paw came out with a big smile, "It's a girl! My Maggie jist had a big baby girl! I gotta get saddled and go tell Deke, if I can find him. You jist stay here, 'case they need sumthin' in there." Paw looked at and said, "Hell you cain't git 'em nuthin' anyway. Jist stay close."

Sophia came to the door a few minutes later. "Meester Max, Mees Maggie wants you to come een to see the babee." Max couldn't get into the house fast enough. He really just wanted to make sure Maggie was alright. His heart skipped when he saw her. She was trying to get the pink and wrinkled baby to suckle her breast.

"My God you're beautiful" he thought. *"Even more beautiful than you were this morning. Maybe being a mother does that to you. My mother was beautiful, too."*

"So this was why you wanted me out of the house," he stated. "How long have you been in labor?"

"Nearly all night," she said. "I wanted to wait until all you men were out of the house, and it worked. If y'all had been in here, poor Sophia wouldn't have been able to move around without stumbling over you."

"What was your mother's name, Max?" Maggie asked him, smiling. *"What? How did she know I was thinking about my mother?"* was his first thought. He replied that her name was Emily, and Maggie said she loved the name. Her baby would be named Emily. Max's eyes filled with tears, and he left the room, happier than he'd been in years. He told Sophia that he would be in the tack room, in case she needed him.

Two hours later, Paw came back, walking his horse into the yard. When Max heard him, he grabbed his crutches and went out to meet the old man.

"Deke's dead," he said with a shaky voice. "How'n the world am I gonna tell Maggie?"

"What? How?" asked Max. "How could that happen? Where's Fred?"

"They wuz bildin' fence, west o' here near th' creek. The bob-wire broke when they stretched it. Th' end of it curled 'round fast, like a whip, an' stuck d'rectly thru Deke's neck. Fred said he didn't even yell. He jist fell down an' kicked twice't." Fred's bringing him in, shortly. It happened jist a few minutes before I got there. Fred was fixin' to come to th' house t' git me, when I rode up." Paw looked at Max with the saddest eyed he'd ever seen. "How am I gonna tell her, Max?" That was the only time Paw had ever called him 'Max'.

Suddenly Sophia screamed from the porch, making both men jump. They looked at her, and saw her pointing at Fred. He was coming across the last few yards, before entering the front gate. He was leading Deke's horse, Dobie, with Deke draped across the saddle. Max told him to take Deke to the barn. They all could hear Maggie calling out, wondering what was going on.

Max was the first to enter her room, followed by Fred and Sophia. Paw was holding back. He didn't want anyone to see his tears, or his body trembling. He was the tough one. The mean one. The one who gripes and gives orders. He wasn't supposed to be the one crying.

Maggie wept for hours. Sophia stayed with her, and Max was just outside her door. Paw sent Fred for the undertaker, then stayed in the barn waiting for them to return. The undertaker brought his nephew, to dig the grave. Paw told them to dig it on the hill, where the other markers were.

On the way to town, Fred had stopped at two neighbors' houses with the sad news. From there, it spread by word of mouth, and within a few hours, people were coming from every direction.

Before morning, a camp of more than eighty people had been set up, just outside the gate. The smells of coffee, bacon, ham, beans, onions, eggs, etc. were filling the air. Paw, Fred and Max went out to join the crowd. Max was introduced to many of the folks, and he explained to several how Deke had saved his life. The women offered them coffee and breakfast. Paw was regaining some of his old self. A woman asked if he wanted some ham and eggs. "Well I'll tell ya," he answered, "I 'spect I like eggs more'n anything else that comes outten a hen's ass." He let out a shallow laugh. "An' th' ham, well, it comes offen a hawg's ass. I ain't never been able t' figger out why thet stuff taste so good. Seein' where it comes from, it ought'ta taste like shit!" He laughed lightly again.

"Hiram! You stop talkin' like that!" said a small grey haired woman, who was standing close enough to hear. "There's a bunch of kids all around us, and they don't need to be hearing you cussin', like that."

"I'm sorry, Eunice." he replied. "Yesterday was jist so rough. I'm jist tryin' t' make myself feel better, I guess." Eunice walked up to him, put her arms around him, and they cried together. After a few minutes, Eunice pushed him back to arm's length, smiled, and told him, "Now, Hiram, you git your old ass over there and have some breakfast, today ain't gonna be any easier."

As soon as the funeral was over, twelve of the men went to the west pasture and finished the fencing. After looking things over, a couple of them figured out that Deke had accidentally cut one strand, of the two, which were twisted together. The lone strand of wire couldn't withstand the strain, placed on it by the fence stretcher, causing it to break.

Some of the men headed to the barn, and began cleaning. Pitchforks, shovels, wheelbarrows and brooms were churning the dust inside, and rakes, along with more shovels, were spreading the piles of debris on the outside. In a short time, the barn was in top shape. A man noticed the leather repair work Max had left on the table.

"Who's been doin' the leather work?" he asked.

"Well, I started on some of it yesterday," Max said. "But that was before . . . . before everything else came up. It'd look a little better, if I could use my arm more."

"Man, if you kin do even better work than this, I got some harness what needs serious repair. A man cain't git a lot done, if his harness ain't working right. I'd pay ya decent to fix it up fer me."

"Yep, we need someone to do this kind of work," another man spoke up. "When you get your arm in shape, you might think 'bout opening your own shop. There's lots of us that can patch things up, temporary, but speaking for myself, I'd rather pay someone to do it right."

It was something for Max to think about. He really didn't want to leave these people he'd come to love. *"Love,"* he thought. *"Yes, I do love this family. I even loved Deke. Damn! He never even found out that he was a father. Why did he leave? What's poor Maggie going to do, now? I can't leave for a while, not until I know she'll be alright."*

"I'll think about it." he told the men. "I'm staying here, anyway, to help Paw, I mean Hiram, and Fred, until I'm sure they can keep a handle on things. I want to make sure Maggie and the baby will be alright, too. It's going to be hard on them all, for a while.

"The doc says he'll take the cast off my arm next week, the leg ain't healing as quick, so it'll be a couple more weeks before it comes off. Bring your things that need fixin' and I'll do what I can. You can just pay me what you think the work is worth. I've never been paid for fixin' harness, so I don't know what to charge, anyway."

The women took turns looking after Maggie and the baby. Two of them stayed over for three weeks, until Maggie was recuperated from the birth, and her spirits were improving. Paw's friend, Eunice, was one of them. "Now, Maggie, you're doin' good, these days. Whenever you think it's time for me and Bess to leave you here, with all the day to day things that's gotta be done, we'll go. But we're staying till you tell us so."

"I'm sure I'll be fine, Eunice, y'all can head out anytime you want. You're also welcome to stay." Maggie leaned closer to Eunice and continued, "I'm not sure Paw really want's you to go, though. He's been bathing every two days, since you've been here. In my whole life, he's never been so clean," she giggled. "I never realized the smell wasn't really just a part of him. I know you two have been friends for years, but I do believe he's *plumb smitten*".

"Maybe it is time for me to go, Maggie," Eunice said. "Sophia will be here to help out anyway, and Emily is a strong, beautiful baby." She looked mischievously at Maggie and asked, "Do you think Hiram would take me home? You know it's a pretty long drive, in a buggy. He just might have to spend the night, and come back tomorrow."

"He'll gripe about it, but he'll also have the buggy ready as soon as you say 'let's go'. Maggie smiled and added, "Be sure he takes his bath, tonight. He's been working on the corral fence today, he'll need one."

Paw, Eunice, and Bess left about an hour later. Bess lived the closest, so they were going to drop her off, before heading to Eunice's.

When Max's casts were removed, he fixed a bunk in the barn. Fred was gone most of the time, and he didn't feel like it was right spending the night in the house with Maggie, now that Deke wasn't with her. He walked with a limp now, one that would be with him for the rest of his life. His leather repair work was increasing, and he was making pretty good money. Sometimes, he would take whatever the customer had, for his pay. It may be chickens, vegetables, hay or other things.

One day, he took two bolts of material, for repairing a saddle, and gave it to Maggie. She was excited to get it, and hugged him close.

As she released him, she said, "Thank you, Max, you're so considerate. It's beautiful material. I'll make matching dresses for Emily and me. Would you like a shirt to match?" There was that old twinkle in her eye. The last time he saw it was in her room, right after Emily had been born.

"No thanks," he said. He shook his finger at her, and said "I think a pink and yellow shirt would get me thrown out of the bar, maybe the whole town." The fact was, Max hadn't been in a bar since he left San Antonio. "Besides, as fast as Emily's growing, you'll have to make another one every few months."

A whimper from a tiny voice made Max and Maggie tear their eyes from each other. Maggie crossed the room, picked up her daughter, and returned to Max. "You want to hold her?" she asked.

"I haven't held a baby since my sister's daughter was born." he said. "That little one is about fourteen or fifteen, now. I may have forgotten how. *BUT*, the answer is *YES*, I would love to hold her." *"There it is again."* he thought. *". . . Love . . . I've thought of that word more in the last two months, than all the rest of my life put together."*

Emily looked up at him and smiled. He glanced at Maggie and noticed that she was smiling and looking at him, not the baby. He couldn't help but smile back. Then he raised Emily up, kissed her on both cheeks and said, "I love you, Emily. If your mother will let me, I'll be your Uncle Max. All the boys who come 'round to court you will have to come thru me first. Only the good ones will have a chance. And they better be very damn good, too."

Maggie put her arms around Max and Emily. "I have a better idea," she took a deep breath and exhaled, "Why don't you be her daddy, instead?" She kissed Max on the cheek, and took Emily back to her crib. She returned to Max, who was standing and shaking in his boots. She took his hands in hers and looked him directly in the eyes, "I'll never find a better man than you, Max Sanders. I've done lots of thinking. My baby needs a father, I need a husband, you need a family. I know it hasn't been long, but Deke would have approved. He liked you, and knew you were an good, honest man. Fred and Paw, both, have told me they want you to stay. Besides, you love me and Emily, I can see it every time you look at us. And I love you, Max. I grew to love Deke, but it wasn't the same. I knew I was in love with you the second week you were here." She bent forward and kissed him, this time on the lips. "Max? . . . . Max?"

Max wrapped his arms around Maggie and held her as tight as he could. "God yes, I love you, Maggie. I can't believe this. The first time I saw Emily, I wished she were mine. Yes, I'll be her daddy. Yes, I'll be your husband . . . . But do I have to be related to Paw?"

EPILOGUE

Paw came back home three weeks later. Eunice was with him. From the buggy seat he yelled out, "I took this ol' woman home, but, damned if she didn't come right back! Says she'll be staying in my bedroom, too! Guess we better send Fred fer the preacher, we don't need no bad talkin' goin' on."

Maggie, holding Max's hand, called right back, "The preacher just left, Paw, but I think Fred can catch him."

The Smoke Creek Watermelon Festival

Mickey Roberts rode his line-backed dun into town just before noon. Some kind of celebration was going on, all the way down the main street. *'It's too late for the Fourth of July, and too early for Thanksgiving.'* he thought, *'Must be some sort of county fair.'*

"Hey pardner!" someone called to him, "Better git outta the road. The race is 'bout to start. Those drunk bastards'll run over yer ass if yer in the way, . . . they don' care 'bout nobody." The man took off running to the other side of the street, dodged another horse, and jumped onto the boardwalk before slowing down.

Mickey guided his horse into an alley, next to a saloon, dismounted and tied her to a ring, anchored into the building's wall. After making sure everything on his horse was secure, he moved back to the walk, in front of the saloon.

There was a crowd gathering on both sides of the street, mostly watching toward the south, as if they were expecting to see something, at anytime.

"What's goin' on?" he asked a skinny cowboy who was leaning against a porch post.

"You mus' be a stranger," was the cowboy's response, "It's 'bout time fer the melon wagon race. If you ain't never seen a bunch of watermelon wagons in a race fer a two hunnert dollar prize, then yer in fer a time. All the biznesses in Smoke Creek git's the money up each year, 'n the one thet finishes first, wins, *if* he still has all his melons. If he loses any of 'em, he still has to have more'n the the man behind 'im.

"The thing thet makes it real innerestin' is, the wagon drivers gotta drink a pint of good West Virginny rye, a half hour 'fore they start. I'll tell ya, mister, I seen some of the dad-burndest things happen.

"Las' year, Hopper James didn' make thet corner right down there," the man laughed and pointed at an intersection about forty yards south of where they were standing. "He was in the lead, but he wound up smashin' in to thet water trough, 'n his watermelons went sailin' 'n rollin' all over the street. The other wagons behind 'im slid thru all thet mess, but two more of 'em got smashed up, too. The las' two wagons was the only ones to finish the race, but the *first* one whut crossed the line, had lost three melons. So ol' Pop Schultz finished las', but won the two hunnert dollars, cuz he never lost no melons."

The cowboy chuckled and continued, "You ortta seen all them kids run down yonder 'n start grabbin' chunks of watermelon. Hopper was one mad sumbitch, too. He started yellin' and swattin' at them kids, 'n their daddys run down there 'n slapped the shit out of 'im. Whut the hell wuz he gonna do with all them busted melons, anyways?

"After them daddys got his 'tenshun', one of them little farts hit Hopper in the back of the haid with a big chunk of thet sticky shit." The cowboy laughed again, shook his head, and moved closer to the edge of the street.

Mickey heard a shot from several blocks away. The crowd backed away from the packed dirt street, filling the board walkways, crowding into stores with large glass windows, climbing onto balconies and rooftops. Several were pointing toward the south end of town, where the watermelon haulers would be coming from. The noise of the teams, wagons and drivers could be heard above the cheering. Money was being exchanged, as bets were being placed on the outcome of the race.

As the teams came into view, the noise of the crowd got louder and continued escalating as they drew nearer. Six farmers entered the race this year, with the newcomer leading the way up main street.

Mickey thought to himself, *'People will make a contest out of anything. I've never heard of a watermelon wagon race, but there has to be hundreds of extra people in this little town, today. They even get the drivers drunk first. Hell, I'd have to be drunk before I'd try something like this.'*

The wagons were flying by in front the saloon when several melons fell from the wagon running second. As soon as the driver realized he lost part of his load, he whipped his team harder, trying to catch, and bump the frontrunner. It was no use, though, that lucky driver was already crossing the finish line, a block away.

A wheel came off the fourth contestant's wagon, causing the fifth and sixth to lose portions of their loads, while swerving to miss his rig.

Mickey estimated twenty-five to thirty big, dark green, Black Diamond watermelons were lying in the street, busted and splattered, over a one block area.

Scores of children, and others, picked up chunks of wet, sticky, watermelon and started eating the sweet, red treat. It became more fun when pieces started flying through the air. The 'food fight' was on.

'It's almost like they're starving,' Mickey thought, *'but, I think it's just part of the party. If the driver of that first team drank a pint of whiskey, he damn sure holds his liquor well. He never wiggled that rig an inch, coming through this town.'*

"Well, mister," the voice from behind him made Mickey jump, "Whut'cha think? Wuz thet a race er not? Ol' Hopper los' agin this year, but leastwise he didn' wreck his rig. The crazy ol' fart got beat by a snot-nose kid. Thet boy ain't but seventeen, but he kin shore drive a team o' hosses."

Mickey told the man, the same skinny cowboy he'd talked to earlier, that he never thought he would ever see a race, involving watermelon haulers.

"Well, this here's probly the only place y'll ever see one. They's several places here, in Indian Territory, thet grows good watermelons, but the bes' is right here in Smoke Creek. We do this here shindig ever' year, when they gits ripe. They got a co-mit-tee thet loads all the wagons the same, an' watches the drivers, so's they don' cheat. Here comes Dink now, he's the kid whut won. I'm Chollie Denton." The cowboy gave Mickey a firm handshake and said, "Now, my name don't have no "r" in it. Some folks think I jist cain't say 'Charlie' right, but it's C-h-o-l-l-i-e. I'll buy ya a drink, if we kin git a table, 'fore the bar fills up."

Mickey agreed, introduced himself, and the two found a table near the front window of the saloon. When Dink came through the batwing doors, cheers went up and drinks were being offered to the boy from several customers. Dink thanked them, but told them he could only drink when his paw told him it was alright. He then made his way through the crowd to Mickey's table.

"Mick," Chollie had already abbreviated Mickey's name, "this here is my youngest boy, Dink. This here's Mick Roberts, son, he's new in town, but got here in time to see ya win thet race. Did ya lose any melons?"

"Not one, Paw," the boy replied, "Bess was doin' her best today. Shes the best lead a team could ever have. Not one little bump or swerve through the whole course. The biggest problem I had, was gittin' the wagon stopped fast enough to git off and piss, 'fore I wet in my overalls. Thet rye whiskey run through me purty fast." Grinning at his father, he added, "I think Hopper's pissed at me, though."

"Yeah, well, don't you worry 'bout Hopper, soon's the whiskey wears off, he'll be fine. Good thing I done taught you boys how to hol' yer likker. Ya run a good race, son, yer ol' daddy's proud of ya.

"Now, we need to git down to Clyde's, so's we kin see who growed the bes' melons this year. Ya comin, Mick?"

Mickey accompanied the men two blocks up the street, where long tables were set up in the middle of First Street. Nine judges were tasting slices of watermelons, which were grown by a total of eleven farmers.

Most of the produce grown here, in the rich, fertile dirt of North Central Indian Territory, would be hauled to Dodge City or Wichita, where it would be shipped back east, by rail. It would be another fifteen to twenty years before Oklahoma would become a state. Things like railheads, stage lines and commercial haulers were not available, so the farmers had to do their own hauling. Most were friends and were constantly helping each other with planting, harvest and shipping.

As soon as the judging was completed, all the melons from the race-winning wagon were to be sliced and eaten by the crowd. Hopper James had to settle for second place in the race, but was awarded first place for 'best watermelon of 1889.' He told the slicing crew to unload his wagon, instead of Dink's. "These here good folks d'serve t' eat th' best." he announced, "I got plenty more fer shippin'. Now c'mon, le's git 'em unloaded."

As The Smoke Creek Watermelon Festival progressed throughout the day, Chollie talked Mickey into participating in two riding events, and the turkey shoot.

Because all men think they can out-shoot anyone else, more than one hundred-forty men took part in the turkey shoot. The organizers were experienced in this event, and had four elimination rounds going, at one time. Only top qualifiers would advance to the next level of competition. Mickey won ten dollars for placing fifth in the final round. He estimated that he'd used about eleven dollars worth of ammunition. His shoulder was going to be sore as hell for the next few days, but he couldn't remember the last time he'd had as much fun.

He won one of the riding contests, though, and received fifty dollars for that one. The event was called 'pick-up and shoot.' There were four rounds, where a rider ran his horse in a straight line, leaned down, picked up his pistol, and shot at a plate at the far end of the run. In round one, the rider had to pick up his gun from the top of a fifty-gallon beer barrel; round two, from a thirty-gallon whiskey keg; round three, from a nail keg; round four, from the ground.

Mickey was flawless in his performance. The town's marshal introduced himself, and told Mickey "If you need a job, you might think about bein' a lawman. I could sure use someone that kin ride 'n shoot like you." Mickey thanked the man, told him 'no', but was willing to help out occasionally, if needed.

As dusk settled in on Smoke Creek, people started leaving town for their homes. Some had traveled as far as sixty miles to enjoy the festival. September marked the start of cooler weather, although it was still very warm this year. Those who had to travel a long distance would have all night, all day on Sunday, and Sunday night to get home. Most had children, who would need to be in school, on Monday morning.

Chollie and his boys, Dink, Denny, and Henry, joined Mickey, and the marshal, Buck Newton, in the saloon. Because of the festival, there were no rooms available at the hotels nor at the boarding houses.

"If you're wantin' to clean up before the dance, Mr. Roberts, you kin always get a bath at Susan's, she's giving all the girls the night off, so they kin go to the dance." Henry said, "In fact, if your wantin' more than a bath, you might catch one of the girls still workin' if you hurry."

"You boys can just call me 'Mickey'," he replied, grinning, "A hot bath and a willing woman sounds pretty good, but I guess I'll pass on that for now. I need to find my uncle, Johnnie Wilson and aunt Allie. They're supposed to be living here, and I came this way to see them. Uncle Johnnie's got a ranch around here, and I figured he could use some help. It's 'bout time I started puttin' down some roots somewhere."

Mickey caught the exchange of glances between the others. "What is it?" he asked.

"No easy way to tell ya, Mick." Chollie said, "Johnnie Wilson died about a month ago. Allie's workin' over at Susan's . . . ."

Mickey jumped to his feet, knocking his chair over, backwards, and reaching for Chollie's arm. "You watch your mouth, mister, I know my aunt wouldn't work in a whore house!"

"Hold on, Mickey," Marshal Newton, himself, stood and spoke quickly, "That's not what Chollie means. Allie cleans the rooms, does the laundry, and cooks for them girls. She takes care of 'em when they git sick. Every one of them loves Allie like she was their mother. Ain't nobody in this town disrespects Miz Allie. She ain't no whore, Mickey. Now settle down 'n we'll set things straight."

Johnnie Wilson had been ill for several months, before he passed away in July. Allie had sold most of the livestock and borrowed money, with their ranch as collateral, in order to pay ranch hands and for Johnnie's medical care. A doctor from Dodge City made a 'circuit' through the area, every two weeks, and had seen him several times. Toward the end, he even stayed at the ranch for eight days.

Allie was the only one living at the ranch, now, since the hands had all found other jobs. She alternated staying there and staying at Susan's, where she enjoyed being around the younger women. She never judged them, nor questioned the circumstances which caused them to be in their line of work.

"I'm purty shore Miz Allie'll stay over at Susan's t'nite, since the girls won't be workin'," Chollie told Mickey, "It'll give her time to git some cleanin' done, without them in the way. If ya want to go see her, thet's gonna be the bes' time." Chollie grinned, winked and added, "'less ya wanna wait 'til the girls is workin'."

Mickey had returned to his seat during the marshal's explanation of his aunt's current situation. He listened closely to input from the others, including Chollie's boys, who expressed nothing but respect for Allie Wilson. He apologized to all of them for jumping to conclusions, and excused himself, so he could go find her.

Allison Webb had married Johnnie Wilson when she was only fifteen. Johnnie had been the youngest, and last, of six siblings and was just seven years older than his sister's son, Mickey Roberts. Allie, herself, was now thirty-seven, two years older than Mickey.

Tears flowed, for both of them, as they held each other close.

Because of the small age difference, Mickey and Johnnie spent a lot of time together, as they were growing up in north Texas. Mickey also stayed with the young married couple for months after his mother died, and again, for more than a year after his father accidentally caught a bullet in his head, killing him instantly. He had been leaving a hardware store when two young men decided to find out who had the fastest gun. Two other bystanders were wounded, Marvin Roberts lost his life, but neither gunfighter had a scratch, once the smoke cleared.

Allie explained about Johnnie's illness, which had started in his lungs, then progressed to other organs and, eventually, his brain. His last three weeks were painless, but only for Johnnie. Allie was still hurting, terribly, seven weeks after his death.

Working at Susan's place kept her busy and her mind occupied. Susan had offered her the housekeeping job, when she found out about Allie's financial situation, before Johnnie died.

Many people in Smoke Creek had looked down on Susan Cottrell and her 'employees', because of their occupation. It really didn't bother Susan much, but she had taken note of the fact, the Wilsons always had a smile and a warm greeting for her, and her girls. Although some of the women in town thought it was improper for Allie to be working at the brothel, she never felt like her morals, nor self esteem were compromised.

Mickey asked if there was anything he could do to help with cleaning, and Allie told him, "No, I've never had much luck having a man help, when it comes to cleaning. You fellas just have a knack of getting in the way, or finding a way to make a mess get bigger. You go to the back room, get a bath, and go to the street dance. It's always lots of fun. After the dance, we'll go out to the ranch, I'll be through with my chores here by then. Besides, I need to get you out of here before one of these girls find a good looking man in my room. She might just forget she's off duty and try to make a paying customer out of you."

Four days after arriving at the Rocking-W, Mickey used his own money to pay off Allie's five hundred dollar note at the local bank. The banker told him that he had loaned her the money, interest-free, and had no intention of holding her to a due date. "Your aunt is a fine woman, Mr. Roberts." he told Mickey, "She and Johnnie have been very good customers since the day we opened this bank, nine years ago. I would have loaned her the money from my own pocket, but she insisted on a note. You want the paperwork, or you just want me to tear it up?"

Mickey told the man to tear it up, and thanked him for treating Allie so kindly.

The banker also gave him the names and directions to two ranchers, who would give him an honest deal on cattle, to replenish the stock Allie had sold. Within a month, the Rocking-W was, again, a working cattle ranch. Mickey had hired Chollie's two youngest boys to help with the branding, de-horning, and castrating the young bulls. Making steers out of them would produce more meat in less time.

"Where'd you learn to work cattle, Mick?" Denny asked. He and Dink had started using the shorter name, which their father used. "I never seen a knife man as quick as you. Them boys barely hit the ground and they ain't boys no more."

"Yeah, Mick," Dink said, "You may need to use that knife on Denny. Either that, or the de-horner. He's gonna git in some bad trouble one of these days. He thinks he has to poke every thing wearing a skirt. Paw says Denny would hump a pile of rocks if he thought there was a female lizard in it."

Mickey chuckled and said, "That's the first time I've heard that one. Knowing your paw, he was probably talking from experience, especially seeing how skinny Denny is."

Dink couldn't help but hooraw his big brother, "Yeah Denny! You do look like you got some lizard blood in ya. Haw!"

"But, to answer your question," Mickey continued, "I learned most of my riding, shooting, and knife skills from the Comanche. I found a hurt boy near a stream in the Ouachita Mountains, about eleven or twelve years ago. I was 'bout twenty-two or twenty-three at the time, I guess. I took care of Crow Wing for a week, or so, then took him to a village I knew about. It wasn't his village, but the People took both of us to his family in Montague County, Texas.

"Crow Wing had broken a leg, when he fell into a swift water stream. The hunting party couldn't find him, and left, thinking he had been killed.

"His family gave me a lodge, two horses, knives, skins for clothing, ... and a wife to make the clothes for me. I lived with the Comanche for three years, until White Doe died with the pox. Twenty-six men, plus me, had ridden to San Antonio, for talks with the B.I.A. (Bureau of Indian Affairs) We were gone for nearly a month and the disease hit the camp right after we left. Nineteen People died, and probably fifty more were left with bad scars.

"Anyway, she was expecting a baby and it was just too much for me to stay there without her, so I decided to move on. Since then, I mostly worked cattle drives to Kansas City, and did some prospecting in the Rockies. Last spring, when I went to see Crow Wing and his family, I found out that he's a daddy now.

"It made me start thinking 'bout my own family, that's why I came here to see my Uncle Johnnie and Aunt Allie. Now that he's gone, it's just me and some cousins, scattered over Texas. It's a shame Aunt Allie doesn't have any kids, it'd probably help her get along better."

The small buckboard came rolling across the pasture, and pulled up to the three tired cowboys. "Anybody ready for some dinner?" Allie called to them as she set the brake, "It's fried chicken!"

"Yahoo!" Denny yelled, "Miss Allie makes great fried chicken, Mick. Every time there's a social in town, the first thing we run out of, is her chicken. She puts some kind of pepper, er sumthin', on it that makes it the best. C'mon, cut this'un loose and let's eat."

Mickey had to admit that Allie's chicken was delicious. He still preferred the recipe his Comanche wife, White Doe, had used. He had no idea what herbs or peppers she had used, but every woman should cook so good. It was no surprise that, after the chicken, new potatos, biscuits and butter, there was watermelon for dessert.

Over the next few months, the colder weather found Mickey and the Denton boys spending more time closer to the ranch house, and less on the range. Cows, who would be calving in February and March, were moved to the pastures nearest the house. An adequate supply of firewood was a priority, and the boys were constantly cutting, splitting and hauling wood from the creek bottom to the house.

Mickey rode fence lines, broke ice on the ponds so the cattle could get to water every day, and tried to keep an inventory of stock, lost to the harsh winter. Prolonged freezing weather took it's toll on many of the weaker animals, plus an occasional loss to a wolf pack.

'Can't really be mad at 'em' Mickey thought, 'They're hungry, just like everything else. I do wish they'd move on out of this part of the country. The coyotes ain't all that bad, they mostly feed on the carcasses of the dead cows. I can't move any more to the front pasture, the grass is about gone there. I sure wish Uncle Johnnie were here, he'd know more about what to do. Feels like that ol' wind is blowin' straight off them mountains in Colorado, today.'

He decided to swing toward the stand of timber, where the boys were cutting wood for Allie's cook stove, today. There was plenty at the house for now, but when spring came, everybody would be to busy to cut stove wood, and this cutting would be seasoned out by then.

Mickey was walking his horse slowly, and as he topped the rise above the creek, he saw seven dark figures easing their way toward the woods. He was downwind of the wolves, so they didn't catch his scent, but when his first shot caused one to yelp, the others hesitated long enough for Mickey to get off a second shot. The second, and largest, wolf fell in it's tracks, while the first victim was still wheeling and biting at the pain in it's side. A third shot stopped that action, just as Denny and Dink came running into the open.

"Wow!" the first yell came from Dink, "Good shootin', Mick. Hell, we didn't even know they wuz out here. We'z only fifty feet, or so, inside th' tree line. Ya think they wuz sneakin' up on Denny? He ain't took a bath in a couple weeks. Bad as he smells, they might'a thought they had a wile hog, or sumthin', cornered in these woods. Do ya know if wolves eat skunks?"

Mickey was glad the boys were taking it in stride. Wolves rarely attack humans, but it has happened. Now Denny was wanting to skin the creatures, tan the skins, and get Allie to make him a coat, with the fur inside, for warmth.

'These boys are made from good stock, in spite of Chollie being their daddy,' he thought, 'I ain't met their mother, but they must get their grit from her and *their bullshit from Chollie. Good combination, I reckon. If I ever get boys of my own, I pray they turn out this good.'*

"I've been doin' some thinking," Allie told Mickey when they returned, with the load of stove wood and wolf skins, "When Johnnie and I built this house, we thought we'd be having children. So . . . We have three bedrooms, and two aren't being used. I don't see a need of heating the bunkhouse, when there's room for all of us in here. You can sleep in the smaller room, and the boys can take the other. My room is on the other side of the house, so I'll still have my privacy. We all eat and spend time in here, anyway, so you three get your stuff from the bunkhouse while I start supper. Hurry up now, and don't be fanning that North door."

Mickey's attempt at a protest was cut short, the gear was moved into the main house, and the fire in the bunkhouse fireplace was allowed to die out.

Being in the presence of Allie was good for the two boys. They were, surprisingly, very well mannered around her, and she enjoyed playing the role of 'mother'.

Denny had his twentieth birthday on January 2nd. Chollie, his wife Julia, and Henry, the oldest of the three siblings, rode out to the Rocking-W for dinner, but returned home soon afterward. Tall, thick clouds were indicating heavy snow was on it's way.

"By th' way, Mick," Chollie said, "Paul Diggins, jist west o' here 'bout two 'n a haf, mebbe three mile, quit this here part of ranchin'. He's leavin' nex' week fer Alabammy, 'n he's got a big-ass barn plumb full o' hay. He mite make ya a good deal on it iffen yer innerested. Long's the road stays open, y'all got a good, big wagon t' haul it with. Jist thought I'd tell ya."

A light snow was falling, the next day. Allie rode on the wagon with Dink, as they all made the trip to the Diggins ranch. Allie and Johnnie had been the first to welcome the family of four, six years ago, when they moved here from Iowa, and she wanted to see them one more time before they left the Smoke Creek area.

Paul Diggins gave the hay to Allie, and told her, "You and Johnnie were as good as any neighbors could be. I'll not take any pay from you for the hay. Take every bit of it, if you want. If you know anyone looking for a good place, with a good house, water, barn, and pens, I'll make them a fair price on this one. I got a clear deed on the place, and I'll even let a good man pay it out, if that's what he needs to do. Maddy just can't tolerate this weather, anymore, so we're headin' for southern Alabama."

Mickey, Dink, Denny, and John Diggins, Paul's son, loaded the wagon with the first load of hay, then Mickey sent Allie and the boys home.

"Pitch this whole load to the stock in the first pasture," he told them, "They've got the shortest grass. I'll be on home soon, but make sure there's plenty of wood laid in, this weather's fixin' to git worse."

"So that's the way it worked out," Mickey was telling Allie, at supper time, "Diggins and I made a deal, and the Rocking-W is now almost four thousand acres. If we can pick up that old Jensen place, it'll be one continuous ranch, from here to the Salt Fork river. The bank is supposed to be holding a note on it, and the Jensens are living in town, now.

"As soon as this weather breaks, we'll cut us some good gates and move most of the steers, unbred heifers, and bulls to the Diggins pasture. There's still plenty of grass south of the house, all the way to the river. That sound ok to you, Aunt Allie?"

"Johnnie would be so proud of you," she spoke softly, with a tear in her eye, "He used to dream of making the ranch larger, then he got sick. He was sick for more than two years, but didn't want anyone to know. Now, you're making his dream come true. I just don't know where the money is going to come from, to do all this. There's no way we can raise and sell enough cattle.'

"You don't worry your old grey head about that," Mickey was teasing the woman, who was barely a year older than himself, "I get a little income, each month, from a silver mine in Wyoming. I stumbled onto it about six or seven years ago, found a strong vein of silver, and sold it to a big mining operation. I still get fifteen percent of the profit. I was impressed with your banker, and the fair way he treated you, so . . . my money is being transferred here, each month. We'll be fine, Aunt Allie."

Allie had been wondering how he had been coming up with money for land, cattle and supplies. "Just what did you mean?" she asked, "You said 'a little income', how much is 'a little'?"

Mickey explained that the amount varied, depending on the quantity, and quality, of the silver processed each month. "It's usually around four to six thousand, but it's been as low as twelve hundred, and as high as fourteen thousand. I have ninety-eight thousand in a Denver bank, and sixty more in St. Louis.

"I don't think I'll have to touch either of those accounts, for now, but once Indian Territory becomes the State of Oklahoma, and it will, I'll transfer most of it to closer banks. Mr. Foote was very pleased when I decided to start making my deposits here, in Grant bank.

"After buying Paul's place, and if the Jensens will sell, we'll still have around nine thousand, right here in Smoke Creek. Plus the next deposit is due here on Tuesday. By the way, that account is in both, your name and mine. If you need any money, just stop and get it, it's your's."

Allie was in tears as he finished telling her that, she was the only family left in his life, and her willingness to let him be a partner in the ranch meant everything to him.

"Now," he complained, "Where's that pecan pie Dink told me about, before they went out to hay the horses?"

The Salt Fork of the Arkansas river was an unpredictable stream. Originating in northwestern Indian Territory, it flowed east, through a barren plain the locals called the Great Salt Plains, then continued east until joining the Arkansas River, near the Osage reservation. The water contained too much salt for human consumption, but the cattle had no problem with it.

The Cherokee Indians, who controlled most of the northern third of the territory, didn't particularly like the salty river. Consequently, they had sold most of the land, for two miles across, on both sides. The area included the Rocking-W. Towns and ranches outside that specified area, had to lease from the Cherokees.

Smoke Creek was originally on leased land, but when the Indians were convinced that it was prosperous enough to be a permanent settlement, they allowed the townspeople to buy the land. Most of the residents traded, readily, with the Native Americans.

Paul Diggins had dug three water wells and built windmills to pump cold, pure water from the ground. One was near the house, the other two were in pastures. The third pasture had access to water from the Salt Fork. The well water, in this area, was shallow, cold and sweet. The windmills were built in a manner that all the pipelines would drain, when not in use. This kept the lines from freezing, which could cause breaks, waste and other damage.

Hand dug ponds, or 'tanks' as they were called, were situated in the pastures, to receive well water from the windmills, when needed. However, their use was limited to times when rainfall didn't provide enough water.

Except for the one at the ranch house. A wooden cistern had been built to hold well water, but a spigot was installed on one side of a pipe, where fresh water could be drawn at anytime. This windmill, which was more modern, had a clutch, which could 'kick' the fan in or out of gear, and let it freely spin freely when not pumping water.

"I'll tell ya one thang, Mick," Chollie had ridden out to see what improvements Mickey and his two boys had done to the Diggins place, over the winter, "Paul damn shore knowed how t' fix his waterworks. It's a shame his ol' lady jist didn' like it here. It's a fine home."

"Yeah, it is a nice place," Mickey replied, "Me and your boys have been stayin' with Allie long enough. I'm thinking' I'll move my stuff here, and Denny 'n Dink can move into the Jenson place. It's big enough for both of them, and as long as I can keep them working for us, it'll be handy for them to be in the middle, close to her and me. What d'ya think?"

"Well, at's one o' th' thangs I wanted t' talk to ya about, Mick." Chollie went into a drawn-out tale of how he had passed his good looks and brains down to all three of his sons. Henry was running the blacksmith shop, now, since the previous owner got drunk, 'smashed' four of his fingers, dropped the eight-pound hammer on his foot, tripped over his 'stinkin-ass' old black 'dawg', and fell onto a keg of horse shoe nails. "Ol' Willie's been hurtin' so bad, he jist turned the whole shootin' match over t' Henry. A man cain't do a hellava lot o' smithin' with broke fingers, broke foot and nail holes from his 'ass t' his appytite'.

"Anyways, Mick, ya knows how horny Denny stays alla time. He gits 'at from his mama. Julia's jist grabbin' me alla time, tryin' t' git me in bed. Fact is, she got herself in a family way, well, I reckon I had sumthin' to do with it, too, but that's th' reason we got married twenny-three years ago. 'Course I'ze been faithful t' her ever since . . . 'cept when I gotta go to Dodge fer sumthin' or other.

"I tell ya, Mick, they's a redhead works in a saloon thar, name's Kate . . . . well, never mind, back t' Denny's problem.

"Well, he messed up with th' li'l gal whose daddy owns th' feed store. Ol' man Coates allows he's gonna kill my boy, 'lessen he marries Liz'beth before her belly starts showin'. The pore gal's 'bout as ugly as her mama, but her whiskers ain't as thick. I cain't figger out why ever'body's kids ain't as good lookin' as mine.

"Oh yeah, remind me t' tell ya 'bout thet li'l injun gal over t' Kaw City, she ain't but 'bout this tall . . . . never mind, I'll tell ya later.

"Reckon they's room 'nuff for Liz out at th' Jenson place, too? I ain't had a chance t' talk t' Denny, but I know, fer shore, he's still wantin' t' keep workin' fer you. An' he's damn shore gonna marry her, or I'll kick his young ass.

"I almost fergot 'bout Sandy, over t' Wichita, she ain't all thet purty, but ya ain't never seen a woman thet can . . . . quit changin' th' subject, now, we s'posed t' be talkin' 'bout Denny."

Mickey chuckled and told his friend, "Denny and Liz can live at the Jensen place and Dink can stay in the bunkhouse at Allie's. I've been thinking of leaving one of the boys at the Rocking-W, anyway, so Allie wouldn't be alone. She's been treatin' him like a king, anyway. Fixes him pies, cakes, even donuts! You'd think he was her son, with all th' special treatment he's gittin'. But, I gotta say, Chollie, both them boys are makin' damn good hands. As long as they want to work for us, they got a job."

"Thankee kindly, Mick," Chollie said, "I'll tell Denny t' git his ass in gear 'n git thangs took care of."

Chollie mounted his horse and called over his shoulder, "I jist 'membered, if ya ever need t' go t' Hays City, they's a woman got a boardin' house there, 'n believe me, podner, she gives special service t' her customers, iffen ya know whut I mean . . . . tell ya more 'bout her later."

On the way back to the Rocking-W, Mickey noticed smoke, rising from the chimney of the Jensen place. The weather was still cool, in early March, but, to the best of his knowledge, nobody should even be there.

Two horses were at the hitch rail, and he didn't recognize either one. He tied his own mount behind the outhouse, loosened his .45 Colt Peacemaker from it's tie-downs, and approached the back door. Lifting the latch slowly and quietly, he eased the door open, until the leather hinges gave out a loud creak.

He then shoved the door hard, knocking someone down, and told the man directly in front of him, to keep his hands away from his gun.

"I don't need no problems, mister," the man said quickly, "but you just knocked the shit out of my son, with that door. I'm goin' over there to check on him, so just be with easy with that gun."

As Mickey glanced at the boy, who was sitting back up, the youngster spoke, "I'm alright, Pop, Mom always said I got your hard head." Rubbing a spot above his right ear, he stood and continued, "No need for that sidearm, sir, we're not hurtin' anything."

"This is private property," Mickey replied, "My property. What are you doing here?"

"My brother owned this place when I was here last year." the man said, "I'm Lucas Jensen, this is my boy, Jackie. I didn't know the place had been sold, or we'd gone on into Smoke Creek. Where's my brother, now?"

Mickey holstered his pistol, introduced himself, and shook the man's hand, "He's living in town, working at the mercantile. His wife and son clean a couple business at night. They're probably making better money than ranching ever paid. They seem to be happy, too."

Lucas Jensen apologized for the intrusion, checked the side of Jackie's head, then offered Mickey some coffee. "You might as well have a cup, I guess it's your coffee, anyway. Do you mind if we stay long enough to meet my sister here? She's supposed to meet us sometime today. Soon as she gets here, we'll head on in to town. I'll also pay you for the food and firewood we've used."

Hoof beats brought the conversation to a halt. As the three exited through the front door, Denny and woman were dismounting at the hitch rail.

'Damn!' Mickey thought, *'Chollie said Denny's pregnant girl was ugly. That's one of the prettiest girls I've seen in a long time. I should have known better than to listen to Chollie, that skinny old fart. If Denny wants to wake up every morning with a smile on his face, he better marry that girl. Pregnant or not, some lucky boy will snatch her up quick. That boy is one lucky peckerwood.'*

Jackie Jensen ran to the young woman and threw his arms around her. She lifted the ten year-old off the ground and swung him around.

"That's my little sister, Mr. Roberts." Lucas Jensen said, "She made good time from Wichita, I wasn't expecting her 'til this afternoon."

Mickey immediately felt a rush of mixed emotions. *'What's her name? How old is she? Is she married? What's her name? Chollie didn't lie to me, after all. What's her name? how did Denny meet up with her? What's her name?'*

"Jessica." Lucas answered.

Mickey tore his eyes from Jessica, long enough to ask Lucas, "Huh?"

"Jessica," he said again, "her name is Jessica. That's what you asked."

'Oh crap' he thought, *'I didn't realize I asked her name out loud, I wonder if I said anything else?'*

Jessica and Jackie made their way to the porch, where she greeted her brother with a long hug. Lucas introduced her to the new owner of the former Jensen spread, and explained the circumstances they found themselves in.

"Mr. Roberts bought the place from Elmer last month."

"Enough of that 'Mr. Roberts' stuff," Mickey interrupted, "Would y'all just call me 'Mickey', please?"

"Fair enough, Mickey," Lucas responded, "Please call us by our first names, too. As I was saying, Jess, Elmer and Sue moved to town before winter set in. I don't know why they didn't write us about it. They should have known we'd be coming today."

Jessica looked at Mickey and spoke up, "You see, Mr. Rob . . . . , I mean Mickey, March 19th was the day we lost our parents, exactly one year apart. For the last four years, all three of us have been getting together here, at Elmer's place, on that day. Our folks are buried in that little cemetery over yonder, on that hill. Would you, please, allow us to go up there and spend a little time? Then we'll go to town and be out of your hair."

Mickey told them to spend all the time they wanted. *"In fact, Jessica Jensen, you can stay the rest of your life."* he thought, *"Make that, the rest of our lives."*

Denny explained to Mickey, that he had stopped on the road, to check a shoe on his horse's hoof. Jessica rode up and asked if he needed help. "Kin you believe that, Mick? That little woman was askin' me if I needed help. I could have been a bad ass outlaw, lookin' to do in a innocent woman. She's either damn nice, or damn careless. Ain't no doubt she's damn purty. Anyway, she offered to ride on to her brother's place to git me help. 'Bout that time, I got a rock outta ol' Boots' hoof, so I jist rode on in with her. I didn't realize, til we was here, that she was Elmer Jensen's sis. If I wasn't *be-trothed* already, I'd be tempted to set my sights on that gal."

"I'd really be surprised, Denny, if that woman ain't already got herself a good man. If she ain't, someone's sure missin' the boat."

Mickey offered to let Lucas, Jackie and Jessica use the house, instead of finding rooms in town. They could ride to Smoke Creek, see Elmer, Sue and their children, but stay out at the former Jensen place, as long as they wanted. Until Denny married Liz, the place would be empty, anyway.

They accepted and invited him and Allie to breakfast, the next morning. Mickey had told them his aunt was his partner, and that he would like them to meet her. He would bring milk and eggs, to go with whatever supplies were in the house already.

After visiting with them for an hour, or so, he had found out that Lucas's wife had left him, and their son, for a gambler, in Dodge City. That had been eight years ago, when Jackie was only two. Lucas was the overseer of the cattle pens in the Dodge City stockyards.

Jessica owned a restaurant in Wichita, Kansas, about sixty-five miles from Smoke Creek. "If you ever get up my way, it's called 'Jessie's Café'. Coffee's always free, food's always good. When cattle drives are in town, it's hard to get a seat in my place. But, the money's really good during those times." she said, smiling at Mickey. "A few times I've thought about opening a smaller place here, in Smoke Creek. I'd be closer to Elmer, and Lucas. Heck, if I only made *half* of the money I make in Wichita, I'd do fine.

"My brothers have been harping on me to find a man, and settle down for years. Finding a man wouldn't be a problem, just the *right* man. I've been on my own for so long, I'm not sure anyone could put up with me."

"I could!" Mickey declared in his mind, *"I'd put up with you, Jessica Jensen."*

Mickey bid the Jensens good-bye and rode to the Rocking-W with Denny. The boy would be marring Liz Coates next week, so they would be moving a couple of days before that. Mickey told him that he would let the Jensen's stay at the Diggins house, whenever he and Liz needed to move in, if they were still here.

As it turned out, Allie had met Jessica a few years ago, at the burial service for Jessica's mother. She was sure she had met Lucas, at the same time, but couldn't remember him.

Jackie became Allie's buddy immediately. She had brought some praline candy, she had made, with pecans in it. "I made these 'specially for you, mister Jackson Jensen. The others can only have some, if you want to share."

Breakfast was quite interesting that Saturday morning. Elmer and Sue Jensen joined the others, along with their children. Everyone joked about Mickey knocking Jackie down the day before, when he found Lucas and his son at the house.

The group had a good laugh when Mickey told how a first impression, had led him to believe that Jessica was the girl Denny had put in a family way.

Allie took note of the way Jackie was watching his supply of pralines. He was sharing, but sharing had it's limits.

Lucas said very little, but was watching Allie, constantly.

Jessica and Mickey laughed and teased each other until their sides hurt.

It was over all too soon, for all of them.

Throughout the spring and summer, Mickey found himself needing supplies from Wichita, on a regular basis. He had hired three other good hands, including Chollie Denton. As it turned out, Chollie was an excellent foreman, in spite of his good natured teasing. His sons, and the other hands, knew his ornery personality, and were just as quick to accept work assignments from him, as they were from Mickey. Therefore, when it was necessary to get supplies from Wichita, Mickey elected to make the trip, himself.

On a Saturday morning, toward the end of August, Jessie's Café was a busy place, when Mickey walked in for breakfast. As he went to sit at a table in the rear of the room, a chair leg broke, causing him to tumble to the floor. Jessica, who had seen him come in, was directly behind him with a mug of hot coffee. As he sprawled backwards, Mickey's reflex was to grab for something to break his fall. The only thing his hand clutched was Jessica's dress, which tore at the waist.

When she caught the torn place with her left hand, hot coffee spilled on Mickey's arm, causing a loud 'OUCH' to escape. Everything happened so quickly, nobody was sure what caused Jessica to fall on top of Mickey, but as she rolled off, she banged her head on the sharp point of the broken chair leg.

One of the other customers, a very big man, picked her up and sat her in an empty chair. When he noticed blood trickling down the side of her face, he turned to Mickey, "Watch what the hell ya doin', ya clumsy ass. Ya done went and hurt my girl. Soon's I know she's alright, I'm gonna stomp ya in the dirt."

'Who is this guy?' asked the voice in Mickey's head. *"I've been courting Jess for six months. What' this about her being his girl? She's never said a thing about another man. God, please don't let her be hurt bad.'*

Jessica started giggling about that time and said, "Oh, Bud, you know I'm not your girl, and nobody's gonna stomp nobody else." She touched the cut in her scalp and continued, "I'm not hurt, and Mickey is a friend of mine. He comes in, from time to time, so he can break up my furniture, and tear off my clothes. Now, sit back down and eat." She looked at Mickey, who was still sitting on the floor, smiled and said, "Can I get you different chair, Mr. Roberts, or would you prefer to be served down there?"

Bud Finner burst into a loud guffaw, "Jist serve his clumsy ass sittin' on the floor, Jess, iffen he gits up, he'll jist tear up somethin' else. Better yet, I'll jist drag his ugly butt out on the porch. Ain't much he can mess up out there."

As Jessica started to wheel around to face Bud, Mickey gently caught her arm and told her not to worry about anything. "Please, just go get a bandage on your cut. Everything's gonna be ok in here."

As Jessica disappeared into the kitchen, Mickey got to his feet, dusted himself off, placed his hat on his head and walked to Bud's table. "Let's go outside, sir, I'd like to talk to you for a few minutes, unless you'd rather me 'drag your ugly butt onto the porch'"

Bud Finner was much too overweight, and as he jumped to his feet, off balance, Mickey jammed a finger into Bud's nose, clamped it in place with his thumb, and made quickly for the door, literally pulling the big man along. Once outside, Mickey turned him loose and pushed him backwards, over the hitch rail, and into the watering trough.

"Now, mister, once you cool yourself off, you can dry your powder and we'll settle this . . . permanently. I'll tell you right now, I've been faced six times and I'm still here. If you feel like you need to keep on insulting me, do it now. If you're scared of guns, then knives or fists will be fine with me, too. I do want to warn you, though, I'm half Choctaw, I was raised by Comanches, and learned to fight from the Cheyenne. I don't fight like you do, I fight dirty and I always win. Listen to me closely, now, if you'll just let it go, I'll buy your breakfast and we'll get along fine, from now on."

The flustered man stumbled out of the trough, issued a few cuss words, and immediately tripped, falling onto the dirt street.

"Why, Mickey Roberts, you're no more half Choctaw than I am." Jessica told him after breakfast. "What was all that, bull 'you know what', you were telling Bud? The poor man won't be able to live down the embarrassment."

"It would have been easy for him, if he'd just said 'it's over.'" Mickey then snickered and said, "I'd have shook his hand, bought his breakfast, . . . and rubbed his sore nose."

Mickey explained that this morning was not a good time for someone, like Bud Finner, to laugh at, or insult him. The trip to Wichita had taken nearly four days, instead of the usual two. He had arrived just minutes before heading to Jessica's for breakfast. She listened as the story unfolded.

"About five or six miles out of Smoke Creek, a singletree broke and scared the horse pulling on it. He bit the other horse and it took off, which threw me off the wagon seat, backwards. I managed to get the rig stopped, but it took more'n three hours to find a limb, the right size, to use in place of the singletree.

"When I got to Deer Run, the blacksmith was sick, so I had to fix the thing myself. While the fire, in the forge, was getting hot, an old-timer came in and told me to get the hell out of the place. Said he was the blacksmith's pa, and nobody was gonna use his son's tools. I handed him a five-dollar silver piece, he smiled a toothless smile, and told me to have a good day."

"That evening, I could tell a rainstorm was coming up, so I made camp in a stand of hackberry trees. I managed to get a shelter built with a small fire under it. Allie had packed me some beans, so I got my pan, dumped the beans in, and started them warming. The rain hit, so as soon as I got the horses picketed, I crawled back into the back of the shelter, which had a couple leaks in it. I took the beans off the fire, dug my spoon outta my saddlebag, and looked down to get a bite. Well, guess what. My hat brim had been catching water from one of the leaks, so as I looked down, water poured off my damn hat, right into the beans. Half of them washed out onto the ground.

"Then, as I jumped, my pan slipped, dumping the rest of the beans, and water, into the fire.

"I thought I had put the fire out, but the corner of my slicker caught under some coals. You ain't gonna believe how a wet slicker will burn, 'specially when you're wearing it!" *(The cloth raingear, of those days, was usually saturated with animal fat or oil, making it water repellant. However it also made an excellent fuel. Frequently, a traveler would, actually, cut a piece off the bottom to use as a fire starter.)*

Mickey's head was shaking left and right, his voice was getting slowly louder and he was laughing occasionally as he continued his funny, but aggravating account.

"I wound up sleeping under the wagon, in the mud, with nothing but jerky for supper. Ya see, by the time I got the slicker off, the shelter was on fire, too. I just said 'to hell with it', pulled a wet blanket from under the wagon seat and curled up."

Jessica refilled their coffee mugs and told Mickey he should write the story down.

"No way," he told her, "I'd rather forget the whole mess. I sure don't want other people reading about this big ol' dummy.

"Well, let me finish, girl, ... next morning, one of the horses was missing. Guess I didn't do a good job on it's picket. I looked for it a while, but I needed to get moving, so me and three horses went on in to Braman. It took me most of the day to find a replacement horse. Most of the available stock wasn't worth havin'. In fact, the one I bought was harnessed to another rig. The man I got it from, told me he had several good ones on his farm, so he let me have one of those four, he had in town.

"Anyway, as late as it was gettin', I stayed there overnight. Yesterday morning, I went to a little place called 'Fred's' for breakfast. My eggs were cooked perfect, but when I bit into my pork chop, my mouth exploded. I have no idea what kind of peppers were on it, but if I ever find out, I'm gonna grow 'em and sell 'em for firecrackers. As soon as I started cussin', the cook knew he had given me the wrong plate. I can not believe there's a man alive who would like that crap.

"After the feeling came back to my tongue, I figured out that I had bitten it, too. As bad as *that* hurts, I never realized it for nearly an hour. It's still sore as hell. At least he told me he was sorry and didn't charge me for breakfast . . . . I couldn't taste it, anyway."

"You better stop laughing at me, girl," Mickey shook his finger at Jessica, "I'll dump your pretty little hiney in that water trough"

"I can't help it," she snickered, "If you could see your face and hear your 'listhp', you'd be laughing, too. At least most of the crowd in here is gone, now." she leaned close and whispered, "They're probably out there telling Bud Finner about your 'exciting' trip."

"Ah, . . . well, Bud's probably organizing a lynching party, anyway." he said. "But let me finish, Sweetie.

"The trip from Braman to Wichita was another story. It must have rained a lot harder just south of here, 'cause the road was the worst I've ever seen it. The traffic's gettin' heavier, now, going from here into Indian Territory. I would have been here about dark, yesterday, but I spent several hours helping other wagons out of mud holes. "Everybody headed south was loaded with supplies, furniture, or whatever, but nobody wanted to unload anything, to make it easier on their team. The worst mud holes were right in the middle of the road. If you stayed on the edge of the road, or even off it a little, you could keep on moving . . . . most of the time.

"I stopped just this side of South Haven when it started getting dark." Mickey continued, "There's a cleared area on side of the road, where travelers can make camp for the night. The man who owns the place has a few acres fenced off, and he'll let you pasture your horses, overnight, for a nickel a head.

"I knew I wouldn't feel like rounding up four horses this morning, so I just grained 'em, watered 'em, and locked the brake. I had some hard tack and jerky left, so I ate. Then I crawled into the wagon bed. I was so tired, I went straight to sleep.

"About ten minutes after four, I felt the wagon moving. When I pulled my blanket off my head, there was two kids, probably fourteen or fifteen, on the seat, driving out of the camp. I could tell they were kinda small, so I figured they were kids. I just eased up behind 'em, caught their heads in each of my hands, and slammed their heads together. I think the scare was worse than the hurt, even though they hit pretty hard.

"I wrapped my arms around their necks and told them to stop the team. Then I jerked both of them backwards, into the bed of the wagon.

Before they knew what was going on, I was settin' on one and wearin' out the other one's butt, with my belt. After about fifteen licks, I let him go. You ain't *never* seen a kid light out he did. He even ran smack dab into the barb wire around the pasture fence.

"The one I was settin' on told me they thought some other folks, who were sleeping on the ground about twenty feet away, were the owners of the wagon. Them boys thought they'd be gone, before those poor people could get up and run after them."

Jessica was holding her sides, as she laughed hard, "This has to be something you're making up. Nobody could have that much trouble in just four days."

"Be careful, lady," Mickey smiled and warned her again, "I'll set you in that trough. You've already *seen* what happens to people that laugh at me. You're about to *feel* it, too."

As Mickey started to raise out of his chair, Jessica told him she'd stop laughing. "But just for the record, I'm not scared of you, Mickey Roberts. If you were to put me in that trough, there'd be fifteen of my boyfriends on your back in minutes."

"Ha!" he sat back in his chair and said, "They'd probably be cheering me on, woman. Now do you want to hear the rest?"

She grinned, wickedly, filled their cups again and told him, "Sure, just don't make me laugh, ... I sure don't want to get dropped in the water."

"Alright . . . . I dragged that second boy over to a campfire and made him apologize to the people who were camped. All of them were woke up by the fracas, and I figured he, at least, need to say 'I'm sorry'. Soon as I let go of him, he was haulin' his butt down that road." Mickey chuckled and added, "I'll bet he could have outrun a bullet.

"Now, you have to remember, too, that all this took place in the darkest part of the night. If it wasn't for moonlight and a little from the campfire, nobody would have been able to see anything that was goin' on.

"As long as I was already awake, I decided to get the team rollin' and come on in to Wichita. Then, lo and behold, I walk into my girlfriend's eatin' joint, and fall on my ass, in front of twenty people. How fitting!"

Jessica left the table, laughing, as she headed for the kitchen.

"Well, Lydia," she said excitedly to the woman at the stove, "This is it. Are you sure you're ready to take over? Oh, listen to me, you been doing almost everything for the last two weeks, anyway." She hugged the heavy woman and continued, "I think you'll do fine here, and Wichita needs a good cook like you. But, if you ever decide this town is too big for you, I'd be happy for you to look me up in Smoke Creek. Just remember, you'll have to ask for Mrs. Jessica Roberts. Mickey and I will be getting married next weekend, during the Smoke Creek Watermelon Festival."

"I'll miss you, Jess," Lydia replied, "You've been so good to me. Giving me a job, helping me get my kids and I a home, and, most of all, letting me buy this wonderful café from you. I promise I won't be late on payments. Fifth of the month, your hundred dollars will be in the bank. You're sure you don't want me to send it to you?"

"No, dear," Jessica said, "Just put it in the account here. It'll be less trouble and it'll be here for us to use, when we have to come to Wichita, for business or supplies. And, of course, you know we'll always eat here. We'll be leaving tomorrow morning after breakfast. Mickey will have all my things loaded by this afternoon and he'll pick me up here, in the morning.

"I'm so excited, Lydia, I'm going to be *married!*"

As Mickey pulled the rig, loaded with everything from dishes to furniture and cuckoo clocks, into the alleyway behind Jessie's Café, Bud Finner stepped around the corner of the building. "Get yer smart ass down from there, Roberts," Bud said, "We got some bizness to finish."

Mickey told the big man that there was no reason for anybody to get upset, much less hurt. He explained that he and Jessica had been engaged for the last two months, and they would be married within the next week.

As he climbed off the wagon seat, a boy, about eight years old, ran down the alley.

"Hey, son!" Mickey called to him, "Go find a lawman for me." he pitched the boy a quarter and added, "Tell him to bring a doctor, too."

As the boy took off, Bud Finner told Mickey, "You gonna need a doc when I git thru with ya. You gonna be beat up, an' tore up, so bad, Jess ain't even gonna wanna look at'cha, much less marry up with ya. Ya ain't gonna s'prise me like ya did yesterday. Ya gonna face me like a man, now."

"I'll face you like a man, Finner, but if we're gonna fight like men, let's go out in front, in the street. After all, you can't take much pride in kicking my ass if there's nobody watching. Unless, of course, you don't want anyone watching, just in case it's your ass that gets kicked."

Mickey ducked under the left hook and stepped sideways. He wanted to stall long enough for the law to get back, and let *them* handle Bud Finner. However, Bud's next swing caught Mickey's left shoulder, spinning him into the rear flank of one of his horses. The horse jumped and kicked, hitting the horse behind it. The sudden jolt caused the brake to loosen. Mickey saw what was happening, grabbed at the reins and but only caught the one attached to the lead horse on the left side. As he stumbled, the rein jerked, causing the horse to swing it's head sharply to it's left.

The collision could be heard a block away. Bud had looked downward at Mickey, and never saw the big bay's head coming. Needless to say, Bud Finner's head lost that battle.

The lawman had arrived in time to see the accident, with a doctor just a few steps behind him.

Mickey was able to calm the horses, reset the brake and tie it in place.

Bud Finner was dead.

EPILOGUE

Because the deputy marshal had witnessed the accident, causing Bud Finner's death, there was no need for a coroner's inquest.

Mickey Roberts and Jessica Jensen were married at the tasting table, during the 1890 Smoke Creek Watermelon Festival. Chollie Denton served as best man and the bride was given away by her oldest brother, Elmer. Elmer's wife, Sue, was the matron of honor. Other members of the wedding party were eleven year-old Jackie Jensen, his father Lucas, and his new step-mother, the former Allie Wilson.

The judges declared Hopper James had grown the best melons, for the second straight year. Another repeat winner was Dink Denton, with first place in the melon wagon race.

Denny and Liz Denton showed off their new baby girl, Denise. In a drastic contrast to the outward appearance of her parents, Denise was a pretty baby.

Just before the dance started, Beau Foote, the owner of Grant Bank, mounted the steps of the bandstand, and asked the assembled crowd for silence. He then announced his engagement to Susan Cottrell. It was a smart move for Mr. Foote, her brothel was the most profitable business in Smoke Creek.

Jessica Roberts, her children, and grandchildren operated 'Jessie's Café' for sixty-four years in Smoke Creek, Oklahoma.

The Rocking-W became a top producer of prime beef. At one point, it supplied more than four thousand head, per year, to the Bureau of Indian Affairs, who distributed it, primarily, to the Cherokee Nation.